"Sarah Minton."

Richard caught his breath. Sarah? Which one of them was Sarah?

He stared as the last of the three stood and faced them. Her gaze never left the floor. All of them trembled, but Sarah, if it were truly she, looked terrified. Her once-lustrous hair lay matted and dirty against her skull. Her tattered dress hung about a wasted frame. *If she would only look up*, Richard thought. If he could see into her eyes, he would know if this was Sarah, the girl he had loved—or dreamed of loving. But she continued to stare downward with dull eyes. He inhaled carefully and swallowed the bile that surged into his throat. This was not Sarah. It couldn't be.

SUSAN PAGE DAVIS and her husband, Jim, have been married thirty-two years and have six children, ages thirteen to thirty, and five grandchildren. They live in Maine, where they are active in a small, independent Baptist church. Susan is a homeschooling mother. She has published novels in the historical romance, cozy mystery, romantic suspense, fantasy, and young adult genres. She loves to hear from her readers. Visit Susan at her Web site: www.susanpagedavis.com.

Books by Susan Page Davis

Return to Love

Susan Page Davis

Heartsong Presents

To our dear little granddaughter, Reagan. I wish we lived closer and I could spend more time with you. I love you forever. Marmee

Glossary:

Banns—a public announcement, especially in church, of an
    upcoming marriage
Byre—a barn
Goodman—a social title for a yeoman farmer or householder
    who did not attain the rank of gentleman
Goody—a shortened form of *goodwife*, a term of civility applied
    to a married woman in humble life
Ordinary—a tavern or eating house
Relict—a widow

A note from the Author:
I love to hear from my readers! You may correspond with me by writing:

Susan Page Davis
Author Relations
PO Box 721
Uhrichsville, OH 44683

ISBN 978-1-60260-011-9

RETURN TO LOVE

Our mission is to publish and distribute inspirational products offering exceptional value and biblical encouragement to the masses.

PRINTED IN THE U.S.A.

one

Cochecho, New Hampshire, 1689

Richard Dudley bolted upright, his heart pounding in the dark. The sound that had wakened him came once more—a distant but terrible shriek, splitting the night. Only an Indian out for blood could make that gruesome noise.

"Richard!" His father's forceful voice came from below.

"I hear it."

"Quick! Wake your sister. We must run to Otis's."

"I'm awake," came Catherine's voice from behind the half partition that separated their sleeping areas in the loft.

Richard scrambled to pull on his breeches and shoes. A moment's hesitation could mean death in an Indian raid. He leaped down the ladder, pausing only to be sure Catherine made it safely down in her billowing skirts. His parents hadn't built up the fire, and only a faint glow from the coals lit the room. Richard sensed movement and knew his mother was gathering emergency supplies. No doubt his father had dashed to grab his loaded musket that hung above the door. Richard groped his way to the corner where his own weapon leaned against the wall.

"Stephen," his mother gasped, and Richard's heart sank at the thought of his younger brother.

"He'll be safe at Otis's garrison," her husband said. "It's ourselves we must worry about. Catherine?"

"Here, Father."

"Come, then."

"Take this." Their mother's voice was low and urgent. She pressed a sack into Richard's hand, and he knew it held food. He suspected his mother and Catherine also carried food or blankets. They had discussed sudden flight many times across the supper table and practiced it once before when an outlying farm was raided and the warning came to fort up at the nearest garrison.

That would be Otis's, the closest fortified house. The blacksmith and his large family offered protection for other settlers whenever needed, as did Waldron, Heard, and other prominent men in the struggling community. Their houses were fenced all around and built of sturdy oak, with rifle loops for windows above and the second story protruding over the first, so that attackers could be fired down upon. Richard prayed the people within would be safe, as well as the other families who were certainly running toward them.

The four of them crept outside and headed silently across their newly planted cornfield, avoiding the path. Richard cringed with each step, knowing he crushed tender plants he and his father and brother had worked hard to nourish. But worrying about that was senseless now. If they did not make it to the safe haven, the corn would not matter. His thoughts flew to the Minton family—Sarah and her parents. They were closer to Waldron's garrison. Had they made it there in safety? He couldn't think of her now. Distraction could mean death.

His mother stumbled, and his father reached to steady her. Richard hurried on, taking the lead and hearing Catherine panting behind him. Ahead, the savage screams increased, and a flash of foreboding told him they were running the wrong way, even as his feet took him onward.

They topped a rise, and Richard stopped abruptly. Catherine

slammed into him, and the air burst from his lungs.

"Sorry," she gasped, clinging to his jerkin.

"Look." Richard held her arms and turned her toward what he had seen. A fiery glow lit the sky ahead.

His parents came up beside them and stood silent for a moment except for their labored breathing.

"Otis's is burning." His father's voice quivered with hurt disbelief. The stronghold they had counted on, near the center of the settlement, had been attacked.

"Stephen," Mrs. Dudley breathed.

The two men said nothing but watched a moment longer. Richard's heart ached, and a bitter taste filled his mouth. His brother had gone to the Otis house yesterday to give a day's work in exchange for the blacksmith's sharpening of the Dudleys' tools.

"Major Waldron's?" Richard asked.

"Aye. But we must take to the woods," his father said.

Richard felt Catherine shudder, but it was the only wise course. They dare not stay in the little house or travel in the open. Another glow burst on the sky, beyond Otis's garrison.

"Come," his father hissed, and Richard hurried after him, watching the forms of his mother and younger sister in the near blackness. They crossed the stone wall at the far edge of the cornfield and scurried into the woods, slower now. His father halted every few yards, and they all stood stock-still, trying to quiet their breath, listening. Far away they heard fiendish yells.

Ten minutes later, they emerged from the forest. The smell of smoke broke over them in a wave. A woman's piercing scream sounded, much closer than the other cries, and Father backed up, pushing them against the trees. An unearthly shriek reached them, and then flames burst against the sky scarcely two hundred yards away. A cottage's thatch crackled and then whooshed into roaring, orange fire.

"That be the Mintons'." His mother cringed back against him.

Richard swallowed hard, but his nausea only increased. Three days ago, he had walked to the Mintons' and asked the goodman's permission to call upon his fifteen-year-old daughter, Sarah. Instinctively he moved forward, but he felt his father's strong hand on his arm, holding him back.

"Nay, son. Be not hasty to throw your life away," his father said. "Let us pray they went to Waldron's."

They crouched together, out of reach of the fire's light, until the only sounds were occasional snappings from the dying conflagration and the gentle roll of the river beyond. A breeze sighed through the trees, and the branches above them swayed gently, rustling their young leaves.

Richard's heart was like a stone in his chest. He sent desperate snippets of prayers heavenward. *Almighty Father, help them to escape. Help us all to live!*

"Richard, come."

At his father's word, Richard stood. Catherine seized the hem of his jerkin, but he pried her fingers loose and whispered, "Stay here with Mother."

He and his father ducked from tree to fencerow, silently approaching the ruined house. A few yards from the smoldering heap, his father grunted and stumbled. Richard hurried to his side and knelt by the body he had tripped over.

" 'Tis Goodman Minton," Richard whispered, recognizing his neighbor more from the familiar clothing revealed in the fading firelight than from the man's mangled features. The embers of the house shifted, and a sudden burst of light showed more than he wanted to see—the bloody head, relieved of its scalp and bashed in mercilessly. Richard turned away and retched.

Father touched his arm gently and pointed. "His wife is yon."

Richard inhaled deeply and scooted toward the prone form, keeping low. Her outer skirt had been torn away—textiles were one of the first things savages looted. Or perhaps she had fled the house without it in her terror. Her petticoats were tangled about her ankles, and she, too, had been scalped. Fighting horror, Richard reached for her wrist to check for a pulse. People were known to have survived scalping before, but Goody Minton's life had seeped away.

His father crouched beside him, and Richard whispered, "She's gone."

"Pity. The savages are between us and Waldron's now. We must hide until morn."

"Sarah—"

His father clapped his shoulder. "No, son. She's with her parents in glory, or she's been taken."

"But she and her sister could be lying nearby, needing help."

His father hesitated and looked around. "See you any others?"

Richard peered all about, wishing one moment to find her and hoping desperately the next that he would not discover her mutilated like her parents.

"Nay."

"If it's quiet, we'll return at first light," his father said. "Come. We've others to think about."

His father faded into the darkness, back toward the trees where they'd left Mother and Catherine. Richard hated to leave the spot. He rose and flitted to the fence. Goodman Minton's byre had burned, too, and the animals were likely stolen or running loose. Quickly he circled the ruins of the buildings. The house was still so hot he couldn't get close. He would return at first light and sift the ashes if need be.

He searched the yard and found a pewter plate and several articles of clothing strewed willy-nilly on the ground. The savages had plundered before they put the torch to the house. He jumped at a sudden movement. A piglet sprang from beneath a bush and squealed, streaking toward the river. Then the night was eerily still.

Cries broke out again at a little distance, and he knew at once they came from the direction of Major Waldron's garrison and gristmill. Richard crept back to the place where his family waited. His mother wept softly against his father's shoulder. Catherine squeezed his arm so hard he winced.

"Any sign of Sarah or Molly?" she hissed.

"Nay."

"Hurry," said their father. "They likely won't come back here, but we must find a thicket in the forest and wait for dawn."

They hurried into the trees, away from the destruction.

two

1694

Five years, Sarah Minton thought. Five years since she had
seen the town. Its contours were the same, but structures had
changed. She shivered. There was Waldron's mill—but she
knew the mill had burned the night she was captured.

She and her family had fled their home in hopes of safety.
As Indians battered the front door in, they had escaped out
the back lean-to, running toward Major Waldron's garrison.
Half-a-dozen painted savages had leaped on them just outside
their door. A warrior dragged Sarah away, and she heard her
mother scream behind them. He had pushed her before him
toward the river. A short time later, restrained by the burly
Indian, she saw the Pennacook empty the gristmill of corn
and then watched flames leap skyward from it. Yet here it was,
rebuilt on exactly the same spot, looking more prosperous than
before.

The men who escorted her and the other redeemed
captives back to New Hampshire from Canada had answered
their questions about that awful night. As she had feared,
her parents were killed in those first moments of surprise.
She had hoped that her younger sister, Molly, had survived
and escaped. Failing that, perhaps Molly had been carried
away by another band of Indians. But the captain had told
her gently that Molly's body was found the next day in the
charred ruins of their house.

Many dwellings were put to the torch and nearly thirty settlers hauled to Canada. Major Waldron was tortured and slain by the angry Pennacooks. Yet his place of business looked just the same now, as though the horror had never happened.

Sarah wiped beads of sweat from her forehead and shuddered. Merely walking into the village where she had spent her childhood brought on a dread that compressed her lungs and made breathing a chore.

"Be ye well, miss?" the leader of the expedition asked her.

Sarah nodded. She hoped they would stop for water soon. The hot sun had made their last few days of travel uncomfortable, and the vivid memories parched her throat even more.

Captain Baldwin nodded and moved on toward the center of the village of Cochecho. The governor had appointed him and three others to ransom and retrieve as many captives as they could. The French had turned over a dozen prisoners in the city of Quebec. They had then rounded up and handed over several more like Sarah from the surrounding Indian villages. Some were from Cochecho, the rest from other villages in the colony.

Their company had spent the last month on the trail—twenty redeemed captives and four negotiators from New Hampshire. One of the men, Charles Gardner, she remembered. He'd been a lad living not far from her family in Cochecho, beside the river. He and Richard Dudley were friends.

Her heart skipped at the memory of Richard. She hadn't asked about him on the long, arduous journey, for fear of receiving another blow. Captain Baldwin's news of how her own family perished in the massacre was grief enough for her to carry. But now she couldn't help but think of the Dudleys and wonder if they, too, were slain. As long as she didn't know, she had the memory of him; she didn't think her heart could bear it if she'd lost Richard, too, and so she stared at the village.

So many houses, built near the green for safety. Outlying farms were always in danger. Several new families must have arrived in town during her absence, in spite of the threat from the natives. If not for the mill, the curve of the river, and the rise of land toward the meetinghouse, she wouldn't have recognized the place.

She plodded along with the others, behind Christine Hardin and ahead of Mrs. Bayeux and her children. *Home.* She'd dreamed of it for so long, and yet her exhaustion robbed her of joy. What, after all, was home when one's parents and sister were dead and the town was full of strangers who'd come to fill the ranks? Would she and the others be welcomed with kindness, or would they be shunned because they had lived among the savages and the hated French? She closed her mind to those thoughts and focused on the remaining short walk to the meetinghouse.

A woman and a boy came out of a thatched cottage and stared at them. More people flocked toward the path as it widened out and became the village street.

Sarah eyed the first few but soon realized she was searching for the features of her mother. . .her sister. . .her father. . .and all were gone! She stopped looking and put one aching foot before the other, dogging Christine's steps.

"Welcome back!"

She looked up and saw the minister, Samuel Jewett, and his wife, Elizabeth, coming to meet them. He'd come to Cochecho the year before the attack; the new, young parson and his family had been unprepared for the rigors of frontier living but eager to serve the people of the village. They seemed glad to see the captives. That countered some of Sarah's apprehension about how the villagers would receive them. She wanted to smile at Goody Jewett, but her exhaustion shortened her breath so that she could do nothing but keep walking.

Captain Baldwin broke away from the column's head and grasped the Reverend Jewett's hand. The line of travelers faltered for a moment, but the pastor turned with a sad smile and gestured toward the meetinghouse.

"Come, my dear people. We shall gather with the townsfolk and see how many of you can be reunited with loved ones."

Christine began to walk again, slowly, and Sarah followed her. Perhaps when she'd had time to rest and to accustom herself to the little village once more, she would be able to respond to the people.

Those lining the street seemed as much at a loss for words as those returning. Their faces were pulled taut in anxiety, their expressions curious but not loving. Some appeared to be fearful, others disapproving, but they all looked exceedingly clean and civilized.

Sarah focused on the back of Christine's tattered dress. She knew her own clothing hung in as bad repair. Five years ago, if a woman had entered the village in such a state, would Sarah have welcomed her? Or would she have hung back? If her mother had stood beside her, she hoped she would have had the courage to reach out and embrace those who had endured the unimaginable. But she wasn't sure her mother would have done so. She recalled vague rumors and hints of the unacceptable character of people who had been among the savages. Did the villagers think of her that way now? She looked into the face of a woman she didn't know and saw her shrink back, drawing her little girl close to her.

The meetinghouse was ahead. At last they reached its shadowy doorway and stepped inside, out of the cruel sun.

୬

"Richard! They be home!" Young Ben Jewett, the minister's oldest son at twelve years, panted as he ran along the path from the village.

"Baldwin's back?"

"Aye." Ben leaned on the snake fence, sucking in air. "Father sent me to tell everyone. They're going to the meetinghouse."

"My brother?" Richard asked.

"Don't know. I ain't seen 'em."

Richard shouldered his hoe and ran toward his father's dwelling. They had reinforced the sturdy wood frame house since the attacks and built a palisade all around it. Spaces between the upright staves allowed them to see out over the cornfield and fire muskets through the barrier if need be. He paused to open the gate. "Baldwin and the others have returned from Canada."

His father turned from where he chopped wood near the doorstep. "Did they bring back any of our captives?"

"I don't know. Folk are gathering at the meetinghouse."

His father slammed the ax down into the chopping block and headed for the door. Richard hesitated. Of course his mother and sister would want to come, too. The tug in his heart was too powerful to wait, and he turned and ran for the village. He passed the Youngs' place and the Mayburys'. Villagers hurried ahead of him on the path. He came to the green and cut across it, dodging the grazing sheep, and saw trickles of people approaching from all directions.

At the edge of the street that passed the meetinghouse, he stopped. Men and women lined the track, and children wriggled between them for a better look. Richard caught a glimpse of Charles Gardner, his friend who had gone with the negotiators. His great height made him conspicuous, and Richard's heart gladdened at the sight of his boyhood chum, though Charlie looked weary and thinner than usual. Surely he and the others had been successful.

He edged around Goodman Maybury and stopped short. A line of weary, dirty travelers moved slowly along the street and into the meetinghouse: women, mostly, some with babies or young children clinging to them; two middle-aged men; and a couple of half-grown boys, but none the right age and size for his brother.

Richard's heart seemed to fall to the bottom of his stomach. He watched with pity as several girls limped along at the rear, gently encouraged by Captain Baldwin and William Gunn, another of the party who had gone to redeem the captives from the French. The young women were rail thin, their clothing ragged and their feet bare.

What agony they endured to come home. Richard swallowed hard. There must be others he hadn't seen yet, who had already entered the building. Perhaps his brother was among them. And perhaps—dare he even think it—Sarah Minton?

"Any sign of our Stephen?"

He turned at his father's voice and at the same time felt his mother's fingers clutch his sleeve. Their desperate faces brought his heart back up to his chest, where it sat heavily, like one of the stones he was everlastingly digging from their cornfield.

"Nay, but mayhap I missed him."

His sister, Catherine, sidled in next to him, her face drawn as she gazed at the new arrivals.

A woman cried out, and Richard flinched. Goody Bates ran forward and seized the hand of an emaciated young woman at the end of the line.

"Be ye my sister? Anna Hapworth?"

The young woman stared at her for an instant. Recognition lit her eyes. With a sob, she fell into Goody Bates's arms.

Richard swallowed the lump in his throat. That couldn't be young Anna Hapworth—but it must. He would never have recognized her. Five years ago, she'd been a plump young damsel of ten who sang at meeting with an angel-sweet voice and chased about the churchyard with the boys after service until her mother reprimanded her. Flaxen hair and rounded cheeks, Richard recalled. This thin, careworn female looked older than Goody Bates—who was three years her sister's senior and had married just last spring. It couldn't be little Anna. But the two entered the building weeping, with their arms about each other and Goodman Bates, the new husband, on their heels.

"Let us go inside," his father said. They followed the other villagers into the meetinghouse and, out of habit, sat in the pew where the Dudley family always sat of a Sunday. The congregation waited in hushed anticipation. Slowly a murmur swelled as people craned to see the faces of the new arrivals, hoping to trace familiar lines in their forms and recognize those they had grieved so long.

The Reverend Samuel Jewett stood behind the pulpit, and the room went silent.

"Good day, my brethren. It is with joy that we receive souls who were lost to us. Since this warfare broke out and the peace with the natives hereabouts ended, we've seen many of our kind stolen and hauled away captive. Those who are sold to the French north of us, we've several times been able to bring back, and occasionally we also gain release of some who have been among the villages of the Indians. Captain

,dwin will now read us a list of the captives redeemed om the French in Quebec. Families may take their loved nes home. A few from other towns will be escorted thence on the morrow."

Captain Baldwin, still in his traveling clothes, a leather jerkin over his linsey shirt, woolen breeches, and boots that appeared to be coming unstitched at the toes, rose and faced the people.

"As ye all know, many souls were taken from here after the massacre in '89, and several more likewise in raids since then. A few young people were recovered at Conway soon after the massacre." Baldwin nodded toward the Tuttles' family pew, halfway back on his right, and Richard knew he spoke in deference of Judith Otis Tuttle, who sat there with her husband. A band of men led by her brother had brought back Goody Tuttle and her two sisters just days after their capture.

Captain Baldwin went on: "Others were taken many miles to the west, we are told. Indeed, some of our congregants may still be living in the city of Montreal or thereabouts. However, having heard that several people of this township were sold and enslaved to the French in Quebec, the governor sent us there, and there we did go and redeem as many souls hailing from this colony as we could with the funds allotted. Indeed, we bought back all the French admitted to having in that area. Welcome them back, my friends."

He looked out over the silent crowd then glanced toward the row of captives squeezed together in the front pew. "Though it be long since these have gone from us, and travel between us and New France is fraught with peril, we've been able to locate some of our own village. Some were taken in the massacre and have been gone from us five full years. Others were taken after, here and in other settlements.

Firstly, I give you Joanna Bayeux, formerly Joanna Furbish of Cochecho."

A woman stood and turned. In her arms was a babe of no more than a twelvemonth, and a wee boy clutched her skirt. Richard tried neither to stare nor to do the calculations.

"Her husband, Goodman Furbish, were killed in the massacre five years ago," Captain Baldwin said. "Be there any of her kin to claim this poor woman and her children?"

A man near the back called, "Aye. She be my niece."

He didn't move from his seat, and Madame Bayeux searched the crowd. Her eyes focused on someone, and she waited.

"Be ye able to give these poor ones shelter?" Baldwin asked.

Behind the Dudleys, a shuffle and stir proclaimed the man's movements.

"My wife wishes to take her in, but we've not much room. Mayhap someone else can take the children."

A collective gasp went up from the congregation. Richard glanced uneasily at his parents. His father scowled, and his mother sat with her lips pressed in a tight line, staring at Madame Bayeux, whom they had all known as Goody Furbish.

How could they not claim their own kindred? The babes must be the children of a Frenchman, Richard decided from the look of them. But that shouldn't matter. Her husband here had died the night of the attacks. Everyone knew that. She had probably married again in Canada. And the tykes were small enough that any strange ways they'd begun to learn could be trained out of them.

Joanna Furbish Bayeux clutched her baby closer and reached for the toddler's hand. Mrs. Jewett, the pastor's wife, stood and walked over to her. "Come, my dear. I'll help you get settled at your uncle's house."

Joanna said nothing but followed her slowly down the

aisle. The man who had spoken turned and walked out of the meetinghouse. His wife rose and met her niece and Mrs. Jewett in the aisle.

"Yes, come with us, Joanna. We'll come to an arrangement, I'm sure."

When the group had left the building, Captain Baldwin cleared his throat.

"James Fitch of Summersworth. He shall be taken home by boat in the morn." He consulted his list. "Elizabeth Perkins of this town."

As the girl stood and turned, a woman cried out. "My Betsey! I did not know ye, child!" A tearful reunion followed, and the girl left with her mother and stepfather.

Next was Mary Otis, a granddaughter of Richard Otis, the town's blacksmith who was murdered and his garrison home burned the night of the massacre. Her aunt and uncle, John and Judith Tuttle, tearfully received her and left the building.

The litany continued, and Richard's hopes sank lower and lower. Several of the redeemed young people had no surviving family members to claim them, as their entire families had been murdered or captured in raids. Farmers offered to take in children and young adults to help with chores in exchange for their keep, and Baldwin and the minister allowed it. Richard supposed they were thankful to find places for the orphans.

Baldwin neared the end of his list, and the parishioners who had not yet found a lost relative remained in their pews.

"We have these four young women left," Baldwin said. "All are destitute, their families having been annihilated or otherwise succumbed since the attacks. Little Hannah Lesley is now but six years old, and she does not remember the attack, nor her parents, God rest their souls. Her father's farm was sacked and burned in '91, and she has lived in a convent these three years. The older three I have spoken with during our journey, and I have confirmed so far as I am able that they have no living kin. If any one of you can give them a place in your home, speak now. Jane Miller."

No one spoke.

"Christine Hardin."

Again silence.

"Sarah Minton."

Richard caught his breath. Sarah? Which one of them was Sarah?

He stared as the last of the three stood and faced them. Her gaze never left the floor. All of them trembled, but Sarah, if it were truly she, looked terrified. Her once-lustrous hair lay matted and dirty against her skull. Her tattered dress hung about a wasted frame. *If she would only look up*, Richard thought. If he could see into her eyes, he would know if this was Sarah, the girl he had loved—or dreamed of loving. But she continued to stare downward with dull eyes. He inhaled carefully and swallowed the bile that surged into his throat. This was not Sarah. It couldn't be.

People shifted uneasily. Catherine stiffened beside him and whispered, "Richard!"

"We'll take the wee one," Goody Sampson called. She heaved herself to her feet and shuffled forward, muttering something about "popish ways."

No one else came forward. Richard shot a glance to his right. His father was eyeing his mother, but Goody Dudley sat rigid, avoiding his gaze. Richard's lungs squeezed his chest until he could barely breathe. He felt sweat drops bead on his brow and trickle down his back beneath his shirt. He wanted to speak, but his throat hurt so badly he couldn't even swallow.

After a long, quiet minute, the Reverend Jewett spoke.

"My wife and I shall give these three shelter in our home until other folk feel led to take them in. I know the Lord has a place for each of them."

three

Sarah felt a stirring in her heart. She was not capable of gladness, but she felt easier—less hopeless—when she heard that Christine Hardin and Jane Miller would be with her at the minister's house, if only for a short time. They were all close to twenty years of age and would have some companionship.

Sarah had developed an almost silent friendship with Christine on the long journey. They hadn't known each other before their captivity. Christine's family lived down the coast, and their farm was attacked a year after the massacre in which Sarah was captured. Even their experiences in Canada varied vastly. Christine's years in the convent were a far cry from Sarah's with the Pennacook Indians. But something passed between them that first day in Quebec, when they were brought before the governor and handed into the care of Captain Baldwin. It was perhaps a recognition of intelligence and commonality.

Jane, the girl who had married a French voyageur, also kept her own counsel for the most part, but she had let fall bits and pieces that told Sarah she was frightened of returning to the English settlement in New Hampshire and the reception she would find there. Sarah had heard her pleading with Captain Baldwin in their camp one night to scratch her married name off his list and present her using her maiden name, instead of as a Frenchman's widow. It seemed the captain shared her misgivings and did as she had asked, for he had announced her today as Jane Miller. Even so, none of the villagers had offered her refuge.

The villagers rose and filed out of the meetinghouse, and the unclaimed three waited for instruction. It flashed through Sarah's mind that the Reverend Jewett had offered his home to three young, single women while his wife was out of earshot. What if Goody Jewett disapproved?

One of the last groups to leave the room caught her eye. An older man and woman, a girl with hair that glowed auburn as she passed through a ray of sunlight from a window, and a young man waiting for them at the door.

Richard!

Sarah caught her breath. A spark of hope kindled in her heart. He reached to steady his mother as she approached the doorway and the steps. He looked taller to Sarah, or perhaps his mother had shrunk and was shorter than she used to be.

Goodman Dudley and his wife weren't old, exactly—in their forties, she supposed. But the hard life they led at the wilderness outpost had taken its toll, and both had aged considerably in five years. Goodman Dudley's hair and beard were graying now. Sarah doubted she would have recognized him if she hadn't noticed Richard and identified the family.

Richard didn't look her way. Surely he had heard Captain Baldwin speak her name. But he and his parents had not moved to claim her or even to welcome her. She studied Richard's face before he slipped out through the doorway. He was older, of course, more mature, more sober. She recalled how his face had looked five years ago. Many times in the Indian village she had called his likeness to mind: his laughing face that never failed to ignite joy in her; his gentle, golden brown eyes; his reddish, downy beard, young and soft looking. She'd never had the chance to touch it, to see whether it was as silky as it looked or wiry like her father's dark beard. Richard had come by to see her once—only a few days before the attack—and had mentioned, blushing and anxious, that he wished to speak to her father for permission to call on her. But today he showed no recognition, let alone any attraction. Sarah's heart felt heavy, like the lump of lead from which her father shaped his musket balls.

The Reverend Jewett turned from his low conversation with the captain. "Well, ladies, we shall proceed to the parsonage, and I'm sure Mrs. Jewett will join us soon and inform you of where you shall sleep, but I suspect it shall be in the loft with our girls. The boys can bed down by the hearth for now."

He waited, as if expecting them to gather belongings. When none of the three young women moved, he cleared his throat and tried again. "Yes. Follow me, ladies."

Sarah glanced at the other two, and Jane gave a slight lift of her shoulders and stepped after the minister. Sarah and Christine followed. The parsonage lay only a few yards down the street and downhill from the meetinghouse.

Just as they were about to enter the little house, the Reverend Jewett stopped and looked toward the green. "Ah, Goody Jewett is coming now."

His smile dawned so bright that Sarah believed he was considerably relieved. His shoulders straightened. "Wait here just a moment, ladies."

He joined his wife a few yards away and spoke earnestly with her. His back was to them; Sarah couldn't hear his quiet words, but his wife glanced toward them and nodded. Then she said distinctly, "Of course, Samuel. What other can we do?"

Her husband said something, and she looked up at him for a moment. Sarah thought she said, "We must trust the Almighty."

She approached the three girls smiling. "I'm so pleased that you are coming to board with us. You'll find us a bustling household with the five young ones. I expect we shall be cozy." She searched their faces. "Miss Hardin?"

"Aye," Christine said.

The goodwife's gaze settled on her. "My husband says the captain will put out further inquiries for you, lest we overlook some family members of yours. So far as we know, there are none, but apparently you remembered someone in Hingham."

"Yes, I. . .had an uncle there, before my father removed to the Piscataqua River."

Mrs. Jewett smiled. "Well, perhaps we shall hear good news after a bit. Come, now. I'll show you the house, and my husband will fetch the children. I left them with old Goody Deane when we heard that your party had returned."

They entered the plain little house, and Sarah paused just inside the door to let her eyes adjust to the dim interior. A family of seven lived in this one-room cottage, and now they were adding three adults to the clan? She doubtfully surveyed the sparsely furnished room. A straw tick covered with linen and quilts lay neatly made up in the corner farthest from the hearth. No bedstead, but that was not unusual for a family on the frontier. The entire north wall was comprised of a fireplace large enough for her to stand in, with the massive stone chimney spreading into a wall that included a bake oven. That at least was a luxury Mrs. Jewett could enjoy. Many of the pioneer women did their baking outside or in covered kettles on the hearth. Rough-hewn boards made the table and benches. Clothing and utensils hung neatly from pegs on the walls, and a spinning wheel and loom claimed most of the floor space in the east side of the room.

Sarah recalled two little towheaded Jewett boys five years ago and a baby girl, but from what their hostess had said, two more children had joined the family since Sarah's departure.

They all climbed to the loft, and she quickly counted pallets, surmising that four of the children habitually slept there.

"I believe we'll put you up here with Abigail and Constance." Mrs. Jewett stooped beneath the slanting roof and picked up a stack of folded clothing. "Perhaps my husband can borrow an extra straw tick for the boys, or we can make a new one."

"I can sleep on the floor," Christine offered.

"Oh, there's no need of that. And boys can take such conditions easier than young ladies."

"We can help you make the extra," Sarah said.

"Thank you, my dear. I've a couple lengths of linen, and more on the loom."

"I should love to weave again," Christine said. "I did so in Quebec, and the sisters said I had a touch for it."

Mrs. Jewett clasped Christine's arm. "Thank you. I don't like to ask any of you to work."

" 'Tis only fit that we do," Christine replied.

Sarah nodded. "You are most gracious to give us our keep, ma'am. We'll do all we can to help you with the housework."

"Yes," Jane said. "And we can help with the children, too."

"If we are a burden on your family, we might be able to hire out and help others," Sarah suggested.

Mrs. Jewett smiled. "We shall see what the Lord brings us."

They followed her down the ladder, and just as Sarah's feet touched the puncheon floor, the door flew open and a fair-haired boy of twelve dashed in.

He pulled up short at the sight of the four women grouped near the ladder to the loft. "Uh. . .where's Father?"

Mrs. Jewett's lips puckered, as though caught between a smile and a frown. "Really, Ben, where are your manners?"

The boy ducked his head. "Pardon, miss." He glanced warily at the three strangers, and Sarah suppressed a smile.

"How do you do?" she asked.

Ben gulped. "I be fine, miss."

"That is Miss Minton," his mother said. "No doubt you met her when you were a little boy, but mayhap you don't recall. And these be Miss Miller and Miss Hardin."

Ben nodded and muttered, "Good day."

The door swung open once more, and the Reverend Jewett herded his younger charges inside.

"Well, here we are, and quite a large family we make." The pastor smiled on them all, and the little ones hung back. He handed the baby to his wife and touched each child's head as he introduced them. "You've met Benjamin, I see. Here we have Abigail, Constance, and John. The wee one is Ruth."

Sarah smiled at the children and wondered how it felt to have three scarecrows suddenly plunked into your family. The pastor took the boys to the loft to rearrange the pallets and retrieve their clothing while his wife supervised preparation of the evening meal. Sarah realized she was famished, but that was nothing new. They'd been on short rations for the monthlong trek from Canada.

Mrs. Jewett put Jane to work mixing corn bread batter while she took Christine with her to milk the cow and Sarah went with Abby and Constance for water. By the time they returned to the house with their buckets, the two little girls were chattering eagerly with Sarah about the rag dolls their mother had made them.

As they reached the door stone, an elderly woman approached carrying a linen sack.

"I be Goody Deane, next door." She dropped the sack on the step.

Sarah studied her face. "I remember you. Your husband is a cobbler."

"Was," the lady said. "He passed away three years gone." She nudged the sack with her toe. "The parson told me they have extra mouths to feed, so I brung some dry beans."

"How kind of you," Sarah said. "Would you like to come in?"

"Nay. There's no need."

"I'll tell him and Goody Jewett."

Goody Deane's wrinkled face crimped into even more folds. "Be ye one of the Minton girls?"

"Yes, I'm Sarah."

The old lady nodded. "I mind your parents. They were good people. Pity they was scalped that day."

Sarah swallowed hard. "Aye."

"Well, ye had a hard time, I'll warrant, but 'twas not so hard as their'n, eh?"

The thought had never occurred to Sarah. In fact, she had wished many times during her first year of captivity that she had been slain with her parents. "I. . .suppose."

"Aye. This life is not easy, be it here or among the French."

Sarah did not correct her assumption or tell her that her five years had been spent in Indian camps.

"Good night, now." Mrs. Deane turned and hobbled toward her tiny cottage, the roof of which sagged even more than that of the parsonage.

Sarah called good night and hurried the little girls inside. Mrs. Jewett had brought in the milk, and she scurried about the hearth with Jane and Christine.

"Mama, Goody Deane brung us some beans," seven-year-old Abigail called.

"Brought, child."

"No, she brung 'em. She told us so."

Mrs. Jewett straightened and pressed a hand to the back of her waist. "Ah. Then so she did, but in this house we say *brought*."

The boys and their father came in bearing armloads of firewood, and they sat down at the table. The hostess insisted that the three newcomers sit with them to eat.

Sarah started to protest but realized that the dishes and benches would not allow all of them to partake at once, so she took a spot on the bench by John. The nine-year-old stared up at her with big, solemn eyes until his father chided him to bow his head for prayer.

The pot of beans had simmered all day in the oven. Goody Jewett served them with fresh corn bread and dried pumpkin made into sauce. The good, hot food quickly filled Sarah's stomach. She missed the taste of meat, which was a staple in the Indian village, but realized it might be a scarce commodity in the settlement at early summer, especially in the humble parsonage. But a pewter cup of frothy milk was set for each of the young ladies.

⌘

"Drink up, now," the pastor urged. "Our cow freshened last month, and milk we have aplenty. When you've finished your portions, my wife will fill the cups again for the boys."

Sarah, Jane, and Christine had not spoken of their intent, but when they had eaten rather meager helpings of food, as if by prior agreement, they stood.

"Ma'am, you and your daughters must sit now and let us serve you," Sarah said softly.

Mrs. Jewett opened her mouth as though to protest, but when her husband nodded, she sat at Sarah's place without comment. Quickly Sarah and Jane rinsed their plates and filled them, while Christine took little Ruth, who was barely a year old, and began to feed her pumpkin and milk.

By the time all had eaten and the table was cleared, Sarah thought she might fall asleep on her feet.

" 'Tis time for the children to be abed, and you girls must needs retire, as well," Mrs. Jewett said.

"I thought to speak with the young ladies a moment," her husband countered. "You tend the children, Elizabeth, and give me just a few minutes with our guests."

His wife nodded. After instructing the boys to lie down on the large straw tick in the corner, she laid little Ruth between them. Then she shooed Abby and Constance up the ladder and followed them to the loft.

The minister smiled at the young women. "Please do not fear me, ladies. I shall not bite."

Sarah gave a slight laugh and Jane's lips flickered in a smile, but Christine eyed him dubiously.

"Come, sit for a moment and tell me a bit of your experience," the reverend urged, and they all obeyed. Sarah sat on the edge of the bench she'd occupied for supper and waited for him to interrogate them.

"Miss Minton."

"Yes, sir?" Sarah asked.

"The captain said you spent most of your captivity in the wilderness with the Pennacook."

"All of it, sir."

"Ah. I must ask you—please do not take offense—if you have retained your faith."

"Aye, sir." Sarah could see that he wanted more. She licked her cracked lips. "I had no fellowship all this time, sir, but I prayed every day."

He nodded. "Your parents were good Christians, members of this church."

" 'Tis true."

He leaned toward her across the plank table. "Did the savages try to impose their heathen ways upon you?"

She stared at him, not certain of what he meant. "I. . .was made to dress like them and learn their talk. But I am yet a Christian, sir."

"Good, good." He turned his scrutiny on Jane. "Miss Miller."

Jane stared at him as though she were no longer capable of blinking. "Aye?"

"You were given in marriage to a voyageur, I am told."

Jane looked away, her cheeks coloring, and Sarah felt embarrassed for her.

" 'Twas not my choice, sir," Jane whispered.

"I trust not. Tell me"—the pastor cleared his throat—"would you say that your husband treated you with respect?"

Jane opened her mouth and closed it. She shifted on her bench and looked down at her hands, which she held clasped tightly in her lap.

Sarah couldn't bear seeing the girl's discomfiture any longer. Not only was a man she'd just met questioning her about the intimate details of her married life, but two half-grown boys lay within earshot. She reached over and pressed Jane's hand.

"Begging you pardon, sir," Sarah said, "but we be greatly fatigued. We know you desire only our good. Mayhap we could share our stories with your wife on the morrow, and she could relay to you such bits as you need to know."

She thought a slight flush stained the parson's face beneath his beard, and she looked away. It was not her intention to be rude to the minister, but she felt he exhibited great insensitivity. Jane's grateful glance confirmed this suspicion, and she knew that even if the reverend refused her suggestion, the broaching of it had succeeded in some measure.

"Perhaps you are wise, Miss Minton." He glanced up toward the loft. "I'm sure my wife can help you ladies with any need you might have at this time. I wish only to ascertain that you have kept your Christian faith throughout your ordeal."

"I assure you I have, sir," Jane murmured.

He eyed her for a moment, but Jane would not meet his gaze. At last he nodded and turned to Christine. "Miss Hardin."

"Yes, sir?" It came out as a little squawk, and Sarah wished she could pat the girl's hand, but Jane sat between them. Christine had been cloistered three years and had studiously avoided the men who accompanied them home.

The parson gazed at her and frowned. "Well, I expect Miss Minton is right, and we should postpone a discussion of your spiritual state."

"Thank you," Christine whispered.

He pushed away from the table. "Go on then, ladies. I wish you all a good night's sleep now that you are back in a Christian home."

They bade him good night and scrambled up the ladder to the dim loft. Sarah was glad to escape, but she knew Jane and Christine felt even more relief once they were out of sight of their host.

"There, now," Mrs. Jewett said, rising from the edge of the straw tick where the two little girls were curled up together. "Be ye settled for the night? If ye need aught. . ."

"I believe we shall be very comfortable," said Sarah.

"Ma'am," said Christine, "we don't wish to put the children or yourselves from your beds." Her face went scarlet, and she gathered bunches of her skirt material and worked it through her fingers.

Mrs. Jewett touched her sleeve. "Don't fret, now. The girls will be comfortable. I wanted you each to have your own pallet. My husband will move the boys over to the hearth, and I've thick blankets for them to lie on. We shall all sleep well, I trust, and tomorrow we'll see if anyone can lend us more bedding."

Sarah lay awake long after the little girls had drifted into gentle slumber. A while later, she heard Christine's breathing change to a steady rhythm. Jane lay silent, over beneath the slant of the roof, and Sarah wondered if she was also beset by horrible memories.

But thoughts of the future loomed nearly as gruesome as her recollections of the past. Richard had abandoned her today. She couldn't deny it, and it reopened her long-standing grief. A month ago, a spark of hope had kindled in her breast. At last she would leave the Pennacook village. She would go to Quebec. She'd been bought back with money hard earned by the colonists, as Christ had redeemed sinners to form His church. She was free!

But now. . .what could she look forward to? A life of serving others in exchange for her bread and shelter, it seemed. The man she had dared to hope was still alive and cherishing her in his heart had refused to acknowledge her. The tears flowed down Sarah's cheeks toward her ears.

God above, she prayed silently, *I am not ungrateful. I do thank Thee for bringing me here. I thank Thee for Thy mercy and love. Show me what Thou hast for me, Lord, and I shall perform any duty Thou settest me with thanksgiving.*

Her tears gushed afresh, and she swallowed against the huge lump in her throat. *And I thank Thee for answering my many prayers for Richard and his family, Father. I thank Thee for keeping them safe. And I ask Thee, please. . .*

She blinked hard, not sure what to ask for. Richard no longer loved her. He'd forgotten her, or if not forgotten, he had at least put her memory aside. Perhaps he loved another. A terrible thought clutched her. He could have married some other maiden. Five years was a long time to ask a young man to wait. He was two and twenty now. Had he spent these years alone, or had he found another companion?

A deep sob came from under the eaves, and Sarah flinched. Jane was awake, too. Did she cry for her lost parents and siblings? Or for her husband? The voyageur had died on his last river trip, she knew. Had Jane loved him? Did she miss him now? And did she feel as alien and misplaced as Sarah did, with only loneliness ahead?

Dear Lord, please. . .help me learn to stop loving Richard.

four

Richard toiled all morning in the cornfield. The fine weather had allowed him and his father to plant early this year, and if all went well, they would have an early crop. He worked his hoe methodically, prodding loose the weeds and clumps of grass that grew up between the foot-high stalks.

All the while, he kept his musket slung over his shoulder. It made hoeing harder, carrying the extra weight, but the colonists knew better than to work their fields without ready access to weapons. This cornfield lay more remote from the village than some. He and his father had pushed back the forest as they cleared the field. They'd begun the spring of the massacre year, and Stephen had helped, though he was only a boy of ten. He'd gathered the brush they cut and thrown it on the bonfire and helped pick up stones and load them on the sledge the ox pulled.

After the raid that June, the Dudleys and other farmers had given up clearing new land for a while. Some families had left Cochecho and gone to Portsmouth or even Massachusetts, wanting the relative security of the larger settlements. Some had stayed, even after their families experienced devastating tragedy. Young Richard Otis, whose father's garrison house was burned that day, stayed on. His father, brother, and sister were killed, and a dozen or more members of his family captured. Richard Jr. escaped the savages. He and his brother, Nicholas, and three sisters who were captured and later rescued remained part of the community. Young Richard

Otis had recently obtained a grant of land in Dover, where he had set up his smithy and carried on the work his father, Richard Sr., had taught him.

The perseverance of people like the Otis family had inspired the others, and soon the men were back at work in their fields. They teamed up to guard each other while they worked through the rest of that summer and harvest.

But one can't go on living in terror. Gradually Richard Dudley had seen a change in his father and felt it in himself, a calm determination. Owning land was worth the risk, and they continued to clear and tame it, always watchful, ever diligent.

A noise startled him, and he dropped the hoe. In less than a second, he had the musket ready in his hands and stood still, waiting and listening.

It came again, a step too loud for an Indian. Whoever it was didn't try to hide his presence. A figure appeared at the tree line, and Richard exhaled and lowered his musket. Charles Gardner had come through the patch of woods that still separated their two farms and picked his way now through the rows of bright green corn.

Richard couldn't help smiling at the sight of his friend, returned unharmed from his journey. Charles's butternut yellow linsey shirt splashed a bright spot amid the green and brown of leaf and soil. Richard lowered the butt of the gun to the earth and waited.

"How's your corn coming?" he called as Charles came closer.

"It's doing well. Thank you for hoeing it while I was gone. I didn't know but what the frost would take my early planting."

"Nay, if I'm any judge, I'd say every kernel sprang up twice.

Your field is thick sown."

Charles nodded. "I thought you'd want to know about Stephen."

Richard walked toward him and stopped when they were close enough to talk quietly. "I hoped to speak to you yesterday, but you left so quick. . . . I thought you must want to get home and see to things."

"Yes," Charles agreed. "But your family must wonder about him."

"We do." Richard eyed him without much hope. "You. . . found no news of him?"

Charles sighed and looked off toward the village path. "I heard of where he'd been, but. . . They didn't bring him forth, though we asked for Stephen by name."

"But they turned other people over to you—ones who were taken the same night."

"I know."

Richard looked down at the ground. Of course Charles knew. "You think. . .he's still with the natives, then?"

"I do." Charles shifted and looked over his shoulder; then he surveyed the field and the path before he spoke again. "Look, Richard, boys that age. . . I mean, he was ten, right?"

"Yes."

Charles sucked in air between his teeth and blew it out again. "Ten years old. Boys that age, they think it's wonderful. I mean, look at you! Breaking your back every day, and for what? A little corn, a few pumpkins, and fodder for the sheep. Boys get off in the wilderness and find they don't have to work every minute. Instead they can hunt and play and run wild."

"Is that the way you felt?" Richard asked, for Charles, too, had been captured but was redeemed after two years in the wilderness. For that reason, he was chosen to go with the negotiators. He knew the ways and the language of the Indians. The governor counted on him to get back captives who had been adopted into the tribes. Richard eyed him with new speculation. He'd known the experience had changed his friend, but Charles had never spoken so frankly about his feelings. To suggest that a Christian would prefer an uncivilized, heathen existence might be construed as heresy.

"When they took you," Richard asked, looking deep into his friend's eyes, "were you glad to be free?"

Charles winced. "Not at first. I was scared out of my wits, and of course I hated them for what they did to my folks. But. . .after a while. . .after I'd got over being scared. . ." He shook his head. "You learn they aren't so bad, the natives. It's just that their ways are so different from ours. It's a completely different way of looking at things. And they wanted me to be their son. They gave me the best of what they had, and they let me do pretty much as I pleased, once I'd got used to their ways and they were sure I wouldn't run off."

"So. . .why did you come back?"

"Well, I didn't have much choice." Charles kicked at a clump of grass that Richard had hoed up, roots and all. "The governor's man came to the village and gave them money and told them they had to turn me over. My new family didn't like it, but they had to."

"You were sorry to come back?" Richard stared at him, unable to think it.

"At first, I suppose I was. I mean. . .for what? What was there here for me? My parents were dead."

"You got their farm back."

"Yes." Charles frowned. "After I came back, I realized all I'd lost. Not just my parents and Walter."

Richard swallowed hard, remembering Charles's younger brother. He hadn't survived that long ago raid, either.

"At first, I didn't want to think I had anything to regret," Charles said. "It wasn't my fault I'd been taken. But then. . . then I started back to meeting, and every Sunday I'd hear the reverend talk, all quiet and soft about God and His grace and what He'd done for me. And I started to think about how I'd turned my back, not just on England and Cochecho but on God. I'd given up my faith, and willingly so. And that scared me worse than the Pennacooks had the night of the raid. It's for eternity." He eyed Richard anxiously, as though his friend's comprehension was crucial.

Richard nodded. "That's what I worry about most with Stephen. It hurts that he would forget us and take on the savages as his own people. That he would perhaps have the chance to escape and not take it. But even worse is the idea that he may not think at all about God now. It's been five years, Charles."

"Yes. I can't hold out any hope to you."

"You think he wants to remain in Canada, then."

"Either that or the natives are determined to keep him. They've taken him away from the settlements and hidden him well. They'll probably keep him away until we stop asking about him."

"But. . .we got those others back."

"I know. Some from '89. Some from scattered raids since then. Five years is a long time, though. Too long for a child, perhaps."

Richard felt salty tears in his throat. "I can't give up hoping."

Charles reached to clasp his shoulder. "I know. And I will say I'm glad now that I was brought back. That God brought me back. I thank Him for that. 'Tis a hard life here, on the frontier. But it's eternity that counts."

Richard managed a smile. "I'm glad you're back, too. I had no idea how difficult it was for you."

"Well, sometimes, even now, I think about the family I had up there, and. . .awful as it must seem to you, I miss them. When I went to look for Stephen, I thought perhaps I would see my Indian family again. But when I came among the tribes, I realized I'd come too far back into civilization and I couldn't go back to their world. And yet. . ." Charles tilted his head to one side and gave him a tired smile. "You'll tell your father?"

"Yes. He may want to speak to you, though. Get particulars on what you did to effect Stephen's release."

"I'll talk to him anytime. This first disappointment will go down hard. Tell him all I've said to you about your brother. If he needs to know more, he can come see me or Baldwin. We did all we could."

Richard watched him walk to the trees carrying his musket and fade into the forest with only a quiet rustle. He stood for a long moment in silence; then he slung his own gun over his back and stooped for the hoe.

Two more hours of good daylight. No sense going to his father now. They would discuss it over supper. It was too cruel. Yesterday he'd seen his mother's face when they left the meetinghouse bitterly disappointed. Mother's heart was so torn over losing Stephen that she could not even think about giving aid and solace to those who had returned.

Sarah.

Richard felt a deep tug below his heart, but he clenched his teeth and kept hoeing. He would not think about the ragged, gaunt young woman whom Captain Baldwin had named as Sarah Minton. She wasn't Sarah. At least, she wasn't the

Sarah he'd known. She was horribly changed. And if the outer transformation was so great, how different was she inside? Would she flush scarlet when she left the church on Sunday, as she had five years ago, just because he'd lingered near the steps to get a look at her? Would she laugh at the feeblest jest he offered for her amusement? Would she let her bonnet fall back the way she used to on a fair June day, so the breeze could ripple her spun gold hair?

Sarah has no one. Richard hoed faster, ignoring the voice that said, *"You ought to have claimed her."*

She must be twenty now. They could be married. Immediately he thrust that thought away. The idea repelled him now. She had lived among savages for five years. How could he even think of sharing his life with a woman who'd lived that way? His hands shook.

"How do you know what she's been through?" the inner voice taunted him. He didn't want the details. Didn't want to know if she'd been mistreated. Just to look at her, he would guess that she had. She'd lost every shred of confidence. She was not the same girl who left here so long ago. He would bury the dreams he'd had of her returning one day. The reality was nothing like he had imagined. Too much time had passed, and the stamp of her ordeal was too deep upon her. As Charles had said, you couldn't go back.

He jabbed the hoe savagely into the roots of a grass clump. He would *not* think about Sarah.

A sudden sound startled him, and he looked quickly around, his heart racing. The shadows had stretched long without his noticing. He ought to have headed home ere now.

A flicker of movement at the edge of the field caught his eye, and he stood still, letting the surge of fear and the urge to fly dissipate. A medium-sized boar was rooting at the farthest row of tender corn plants.

Probably offspring of Father's sow that had escaped last fall. The feral pigs made havoc of the gardens, and the settlers shot them at will, only worrying about ownership if the animals they killed had earmarks. If so, the hunter would take the carcass to the owner and split it with him.

Richard's family was nearly out of bacon, and the hams they'd smoked last fall were long gone. The only meat they'd had lately consisted of fish from the river, an occasional squirrel, and a tough old rooster. A bit of fresh pork would go down well. He inched his musket around from his back, slowly lowered the hoe, and worked the gun stock up to his shoulder.

The shot rang loud in the stillness. Probably he'd frightened the nearest farmers. Ah well, it was worth it. The boar leaped and plummeted to the earth. Richard stopped long enough to reload before going to retrieve it. Approaching the edge of the woods unarmed at twilight would be foolhardy.

Even with his musket primed, he approached his kill with caution, watching the trees, not the boar. He grabbed the pig's hind feet with one hand and pulled it along the edge of the cornfield, walking backward and still holding the musket pointed toward the woods. When he reached the path, he hefted the carcass and walked quickly toward home. In broad daylight, he'd have gutted the animal in the field, but he wouldn't take a chance on staying outside the palisade so late.

His father met him at a bend in the path, also carrying a musket.

"Ah, son! I heard a shot, and I was sure it came from our field."

"Aye, Father. We've plenty of meat here."

His father pulled the boar's ears and examined them in

the fading light. "No markings. 'Tis probably ours, but it's so warm we'd best share with the neighbors anyway. 'Twould spoil before we could eat it all."

Richard nodded. "I'll take some to Charles Gardner tomorrow."

"Mayhap the parson needs meat," his father mused, taking the hoe from Richard's hand. "The Jewetts took in three extra yesterday."

Richard didn't want to talk about the captives. At least not about Sarah. He could divert his father's thoughts from the poor young women at the parsonage with the news he'd learned. "Charles came to the field two hours past."

"Did he?"

"Aye." Richard paused as his father opened the gate in the tall fence then lowered the boar to the grass inside. "He says he'll come round if you like, but. . ."

"But no word of Stephen."

Richard nodded. "I'm sorry."

His father clenched his teeth and inhaled slowly. " 'Tis what I heard from Captain Baldwin. I had a word with him today in the village. He told me Charles went to several Indian encampments and spoke to some of the very savages who wrought the terror here. But they denied having our boy. Baldwin says they lied, but he couldn't do any more than that. He'd spent all the ransom he had for the ones they brought back, and the French were not happy with the insinuation that they were not giving over all they should. Baldwin asked them to punish the savages who killed so many here, but they would do nothing. They told Baldwin he was lucky they released the captives on hand."

"Well." Richard leaned his musket against the wall of the house and pulled out his knife. "Have you told Mother?"

"Aye. She's taking it hard."

"Of course. We all hoped."

His father nodded. "You can't ask a mother to quit hoping her child will return." He laid a hand on Richard's shoulder. "We'll hang that pig and tend to it after supper, son."

Five minutes later, Richard entered the house, his hands and face scrubbed clean at the washbasin on the back stoop and his hair raked into place with his fingers.

"Sit down, Richard." His mother placed a trencher of samp on the table, the parched corn dish that stood them well when fresh foods had been exhausted. Applesauce from dried apples, nuts gathered last fall, and a small amount of cheese filled out the meal.

Richard and his father sat down, and Catherine removed her apron and joined them. His mother poured milk for all of them and then joined them at the table. After Father's blessing, they attended to their food. Richard took plenty of samp. At least their corn had held out through the long cold season, and they would soon have a few fresh vegetables. His mother and Catherine had already gathered a few wild greens, and they'd had one feed of asparagus.

"Richard killed a fine young boar," his father said.

"Praise be! We shall have fresh meat again." His mother smiled on her son. "I was going to ask you to take time from cultivating the corn and go fishing tomorrow."

His father proceeded to tell them all that he and Richard had learned about the captives that day and the futile search for Stephen.

" 'Tisn't fair!" Catherine thumped her spoon on the table, and her mother scowled at her.

"Hush, now," said her father. "God above is just, but He never promised us He would be fair."

Richard stayed out of it. He'd heard his father's pessimistic logic often enough. The gist of it was that if God treated them fairly, they'd all be doomed.

"But those savages get away with kidnap and murder," Catherine protested. "We have to grovel to the French and bribe them to return our loved ones. I misdoubt I shall ever see my brother again. Captain Baldwin as good as told you the French know where he is."

"Nay," said her father. "That was not his meaning."

Catherine inhaled as though she would retort, but her mother's sharp gaze silenced her. "We don't know for certain that Stephen is even alive this day," Goody Dudley said.

"You think. . .he's dead?" Catherine asked.

She must have thought of it many times, Richard told himself. Five years was a very long time. So many things could happen to a boy gone feral. He'd often considered the possibility that Stephen had met his death, but the family had never openly discussed it.

"It might be better than thinking he's living as an infidel." Mother got up and took the steaming kettle from the fire. "Who'll have tea?"

Richard declined. What they called tea was steeped leaves of wintergreen, and he'd just as soon do without.

"Well, I don't think it's right," Catherine persisted. "We've got all these other people back—Mary Otis and Sarah Minton, and a slew of folk we don't even know—but not Stephen."

Richard clenched his fist below the table. If only Catherine wouldn't mention Sarah in her prattling.

"We could have taken one of those children with no families. I could at least have had a little sister or brother."

"Hush," her father said softly, as Mother set a cup of tea before him.

"We'll not be bringing any captives into this house," Mother said sternly. "No telling what those young folk have learned in Quebec. I won't be letting them spread strange notions here."

"But. . .if Stephen were found, you'd take him back."

"Of course we would," Father said. He raised his cup and blew on the surface of his tea.

"Then why shouldn't we help one of the others? We could have Sarah Minton here." Richard caught his breath, but Catherine plunged on. "I'd like to have a sister, and Sarah was always a good girl. I don't understand why we didn't speak for her. She was a neighbor and a friend."

"You don't understand the way things be, child." Her mother sank wearily into her chair.

Catherine's brow furrowed. "Richard, you always liked Sarah. Don't you think we should have taken her?"

He shoved his stool back and stood. "Hush, Cat. You heard what Mother said." He turned and went outside. He knew he'd been rude, but he couldn't stand another moment of her chatter. Why had they let her go on so? Mother usually made Catherine sit quietly at the table, but tonight she'd gobbled away like a turkey.

He walked around to the back of the house, where he and his father had hung the boar. There was enough moonlight for him to butcher it now. He might as well. Anything, even hacking up a pig, was better than thinking about Sarah's plight.

But as he set to work, images of the two Sarahs beset him. Sarah, the lovely, healthy girl he'd fallen for as only a seventeen-year-old lad can fall. And the bedraggled, emaciated, and, yes, unrecognizable figure he'd seen yesterday in the meetinghouse.

Heavy footsteps approached, and he kept working. Father would rebuke him, and justly, for leaving the table in so discourteous a manner.

The footfalls ceased, and he sensed his father standing behind him, watching as he skinned the boar. Neither spoke for several minutes.

Father cleared his throat. "You'll take a quarter round to the Jewetts' in the morn? After you see Charles?"

Richard kept on for another minute, trimming the skin loose from the pig's legs. "If you wish," he said at last.

"We should do at least a small part in caring for those poor creatures."

"Aye."

Father stepped around where Richard could see his troubled eyes in the moonlight. "Catherine spoke of sending some clothing or material for the redeemed ladies."

"What did Mother say?"

"She will allow it."

Richard didn't comment on the fact that he had avoided the question. He'd never heard his parents quarrel, but since Stephen's abduction, his mother had changed. She rarely smiled anymore, and her whole manner seemed harder. Poor Cat! She'd been just twelve when it happened, an age when a girl needed her mother's care. And now his sister had turned argumentative. What was happening to their family?

"Perhaps Catherine would like to go along with me tomorrow."

"I suppose that might be well, with you to watch out for her." His father stood there for a few more moments, watching him work. "Stephen's going has been hard. We haven't spoke much, you and I. Is there. . .anything you'd like to say?"

Richard stopped working and stepped back, looking directly at him. His father looked old and tired. "I wouldn't know what to say," he admitted. "Except that I'm sorry. About Stephen, and for my rudeness this evening."

His father didn't protest. They understood each other for perhaps the first time in five years. "I'm sorry, too. You've suffered with the rest of us." He nodded at the carcass. "You needn't cut that up tonight. Leave it for tomorrow."

"Nay, the wolves will smell it," Richard replied. "I'm surprised they're not sniffing round the fence already."

"I'll fetch my knife and help you." His father turned back toward the house.

five

The sun bore down on Sarah's shoulders as she hung clean clothes on the line behind the Jewetts' home. Mrs. Jewett had kept her boys busy all morning hauling water so that the guests could bathe and scrub their threadbare clothing. While their meager wardrobes dried, the three young women had taken turns wearing their hostess's extra dress and a skirt Christine had hastily fashioned from a length of linen. Christine was now confined to the house in the linen drape and worked at the loom while Mrs. Jewett prepared the noon meal. Jane scrubbed some of the family's clothes in a cauldron behind the house while Sarah hung the wet garments.

Jane's thin cotton gown had dried first, and she had put it back on. Sarah's was still damp, and she wore Mrs. Jewett's Sunday frock, taking care not to muss it. The woolen fabric felt a bit itchy and was more suited to cool weather, but Sarah was happy to wear it, even for a short time. The one dress they'd given her in Quebec, to replace her tattered doeskin dress, was now little better than a rag. After a month's hard journey, it was almost beyond repair, but Sarah had mended torn elbows and a drooping hem before washing it, realizing she might have nothing else to wear for some time.

Jane wrung out some white squares of cloth and carried them to her, dripping. "These are the last of Ruth's clouts." She handed one of the baby's cloths to Sarah and snapped the other out; then she hung it over the length of woven vines that served as a clothesline.

Sarah did the same. "A job well done."

"Yes. I'm glad to be clean and glad we could help Goody Jewett by doing up the baby's things. I'm afraid we've made a good deal of extra work for her."

Sarah shot a glance at Jane as they walked toward the cauldron. "Have you thought about what shall become of us?"

Jane pressed her lips together. "Somewhat. Perchance I could hire out as a dairymaid or a laundress. Although yesterday none seemed eager to take me into their household."

Sarah nodded. "I've had the same thoughts. The Jewetts have been most kind, but we can't all stay here. We're squeezing them out of their own home, and they can't afford to keep us. Still, no one wants a girl who's lived among savages tending their babies or baking their bread."

"Aye, the same can be said of a girl who married a Frenchman and lived as his wife more than two years."

Sarah lowered her eyelashes, feeling heat fill her cheeks. "I'd think your state of widowhood would make you more respectable in their eyes."

"Wouldn't you just?" Jane shrugged. "Seems a dead Frenchman counts far less than a dead Englishman. Help me dump this."

Together they carried the big kettle of dirty water to Goody Jewett's kitchen garden and poured it out on her neat rows of herbs and beans. Although Sarah tried to save Goody Jewett's dress a soaking, her effort was only partly successful, and she ended the chore with an edging of mud around the front of her skirt.

"Now I'll have to wash this out when my dress is dried."

Jane squinted at her soiled hem. "Let it dry. That may all brush out."

Sarah nodded. There was more she wanted to ask Jane,

but she didn't care to embarrass her. She saw that Jane was watching her, too, and wondered suddenly if her companion was as curious as she.

"Did Goody Jewett speak to you this morning?"

Jane gave her a wry smile. "Oh yes. She seemed a bit nervous. I expect the parson gave her a catechism to drill me on."

"Oh?" Sarah blinked and shook her head. "He means well, I think."

"Of course he does. And his wife is a dear." Jane's lips curved just a little as she shrugged. "I answered all her questions. If they deem me not fit to be around their kiddies, then I shall have to go."

"They wouldn't put you out." Sarah stared at her. Where could they go if the Jewetts wouldn't have them?

"I hope not. I daresay Goody Jewett wouldn't think of it, even if I'd denied my Protestant faith." Jane looked up at Sarah. "My husband was of the Romish faith, you see. It's not allowed here."

Sarah picked up the kettle by the bail and headed back toward the house, deep in thought. "So, it's only that one thing they wish to know? Our spiritual state?"

"That and whether we retained our virtue."

The words rather shocked Sarah, and she stopped in her tracks. "You mean—"

"Nothing. Just be forewarned. Our hostess will probably ask you some very close questions."

"But you were married."

"Yes, thank God. But to a man not of our faith."

"But still. . ." Sarah dreaded going into the house now. What things would Mrs. Jewett ask her about her life with the Pennacook? She swallowed hard. At least it wouldn't be as difficult as if the minister performed the inquisition.

They set the kettle bottom up near the back wall and rounded the corner of the house. Entering the dooryard was a young couple. Sarah gasped and halted, recognizing Catherine and Richard Dudley.

"Sarah?" Catherine came forward eagerly and extended a hand to her. Across the other arm, she held a bundle of cloth. "Do you remember me?"

"Of course." Sarah felt a flush stain her cheeks once more. "Catherine, let me present Jane Miller."

Jane nodded and dropped a slight curtsy.

"And my brother Richard." At Catherine's bright words, Richard shuffled forward a few steps and nodded without looking directly at either Sarah or Jane. He carried a bulging sack.

Catherine scowled at him when he didn't speak and then turned back to the two young women. "Richard shot a boar last night, and we brought you one of the hindquarters."

"I'll tell Goody Jewett." Jane whirled and dashed into the house before anyone could protest. Sarah wished she were the one to escape.

"I brought you an extra shift of mine and some material for a bodice," Catherine said, holding out her bundle.

"That's very kind of your family." Sarah took the cloth. "Won't you come in?"

"Oh. . ." Catherine darted a glance over her shoulder at Richard, but he was staring at the ground, his face grim.

At that moment, Goody Jewett and the two little girls burst through the doorway.

"Catherine!" Abigail's shriek could no doubt be heard all the way to the gristmill.

Catherine laughed and clasped hands with the little girl. "Good day!"

Constance reached her then, and Catherine knelt to embrace her.

Sarah looked over their heads at Richard, who listened as Mrs. Jewett instructed him on where to leave the sack. He nodded and strode off around the corner of the house without so much as a glance at Sarah.

"Won't you come in and visit, Catherine?" Goody Jewett asked.

"Oh, thank you, but no, we mustn't. Richard has a full day's fieldwork awaiting him at home." Catherine rose and smiled down at Constance and Abby. "I'll see you at meeting on Sunday."

"Promise?" asked Abby.

"Promise." Catherine smiled once more at Sarah. "I'm glad you're back. And I'm sorry about your family."

Sarah felt tears burn her eyes, but she managed a nod and a murmured "Thank you."

Richard came from behind the house, and just for an instant, his gaze rested on Sarah. She caught her breath, and her pulse quickened.

He broke the look and nodded at Mrs. Jewett. "I hung the sack where you said, ma'am."

"Thank you both, and please thank your mother for her kindness. We're most grateful."

Richard nodded and turned away without another word.

Catherine stammered quick good-byes and hastened after him.

Sarah helped Mrs. Jewett herd the children toward the doorway, where Jane was peeking out with the baby in her arms. Sarah took one last glance at the departing guests. Catherine appeared to be scolding her brother, probably for his lack of courtesy, if Sarah were any judge.

She may as well face it. Richard did not want her. Perhaps now no man in the colony would want her. Prosperous families hired young women to help with the housework and food preservation. But none had offered to house her, so she doubted they would hire her. Perhaps if she went to Portsmouth or Exeter, she could find a billet with strangers.

The hurt Richard's intentional indifference had inflicted festered and brought a bitterness to her heart. For five long years she'd avoided the pain of hopelessness, thinking always that rescue would come, and when it did, her family and friends would rejoice with her.

Not so. Richard had no intention of resuming their friendship. He'd escorted his sister on her errand, probably under duress, but Sarah needn't expect more from him, ever. He probably congratulated himself this moment that no one else had come along and seen him and Catherine standing in the Jewetts' dooryard with her.

Mrs. Jewett approached her after the noon meal. The reverend went to the meetinghouse to prepare his sermon, and his wife asked Sarah to help her in the garden, while Jane watched the children and Christine returned to her weaving.

"Sarah, think ye what ye'd like to do with yourself?" Mrs. Jewett asked as she bent over her parsley bed to pull weeds.

"Why, yes, I thought I'd try to get work," Sarah said. "I'm strong, and I know how to sew and keep house."

"A possibility," Mrs. Jewett said, "though most of the families hereabouts have the help they need or cannot afford to pay. Have ye thought of marriage?"

"I . . ." Sarah ducked her head, letting the brim of her bonnet hide her face. "I'm not sure I'm ready to be a wife."

"Nonsense, my dear. You must be all of twenty."

"Aye."

"Then unless there be some reason, some past mistreatment that has prejudiced you. . ."

An odd way to put it, Sarah thought, but she sensed the lady's struggle to get information from her without appearing crass.

She continued pulling weeds. "Nay, I. . .was not mistreated. That is, I was made to work hard, and betimes we went hungry, but. . ."

Mrs. Jewett eyed her anxiously. "Then the savages—the men, that is—they made no. . .advances toward you?" She stood and rubbed the small of her back. "I regret having to ask you girls such questions. My husband feels it necessary, if we are to help you, to know exactly your situations, so that we can represent you honestly to the community. If a man was interested in marrying a strong young female, he would have a right to know if she'd. . .been sullied."

Sarah froze with a clump of grass in her hand. This was what the villagers thought of her and the other girls. Tales of abuse doubtless ran through the colony. She'd heard whispers herself as a girl. One wife would visit another and drop hints of such happenings over their quilting. Captives were tortured and degraded. The women were so horribly used they would not wish to return and face their families if given the chance.

She tossed the grass to the earth and looked up at Mrs. Jewett. "I know you mean well, ma'am, and I tell you in truth, though I feared such things, I never was harmed in that way. Once we reached our final destination, a Pennacook woman whose daughter had died took me as her own. I worked for her and her family. They clothed me after their fashion and treated me as well as they treated their own daughters. I was less fearful then, though at times I did think a man looked on me with designs. . .not honorable." She shuddered and closed off the memory. "My adopted mother did not force me to take a husband, though this last twelvemonth she seemed to wish to see me settled, for she was growing old."

Mrs. Jewett's face expressed sympathy and a tenderness that made Sarah look away. She hadn't thought about it before, but Elizabeth Jewett was quite pretty, despite the calluses on her hands and the fatigue lines at the corners of her mouth. Sarah felt her kindness to be genuine, and her heart went out to Goody Jewett as it never had to the Pennacook woman.

"Well, then, in time we shall surely bring that wish to fruition, though not as she foresaw it. There be several bachelors and widowers hereabout. Once your captivity is not so fresh in folks' minds, I expect one of them will tell himself, 'Now there is a very handsome young woman.' My husband shall have to turn away suitors, I'm bound." She nodded and stooped once more to her task.

An uneasiness filled Sarah's heart. She didn't want to be handed off to some farmer or woodsman who needed a cook and housemaid. Was she ready to be married, even if it were to someone she liked as much as she used to like Richard? And what of Richard? He had shunned her. He was not the potential husband Goody Jewett imagined. It would be another man, perhaps one much older than she, left with several motherless children. What would marriage be like with a stranger? Bits of Jane's conversation flitted through her mind. She'd lived with Monsieur Robataille, the Canadian voyageur, for two years, and for a good part of that time, he'd been away on the trading expeditions that earned him his living. But Sarah had the distinct impression that Jane was happier during the months Robataille was away than during his stints at home.

That night, she again lay awake. They had borrowed a tick from neighbors and filled it with fresh, sweet hay for the boys, so she no longer felt guilty at forcing Ben and John to sleep on the floor. She had the new shift of sturdy linen from Catherine. Her body, hair, and clothing were clean, and her stomach satisfied with the plain food at the parsonage.

But the problem of her future kept her mind racing hither and yon, seeking a resolution. And if she slept, dreams would come. Dreams of that night so long ago, when she'd been pulled from her mother's grasp and hauled away in the darkness. . .

Below, she heard the soft murmur of the pastor's voice and his wife's quiet reply.

She rolled over. Jane seemed to be sleeping tonight, and Christine's snores rivaled young Abigail's.

In a lull between the homely sounds, she heard the Reverend Jewett say distinctly, "We must ask the Lord to provide husbands for all three."

"That would be best," his wife agreed.

Sarah covered her ear with her bent arm and heard no more, but she started a barrage of her own prayers. *Dear Father in heaven, You know what is best. But please, if You have any pity on us, I don't believe a one of us wishes to be married just now. I know I don't. At least, not if it's to someone besides Richard.*

She sighed. Marrying Richard was not an option. Long into the night, she wrestled with that bleak thought. At last she breathed one last prayer.

Lord, help me to be willing to do whatever You want. Even though I can't have Richard.

six

Richard trudged along behind the sledge the ox pulled.

"Ho!" he called when they had gone a few paces.

The beast halted, and Richard and his father bent their backs to one of their hardest chores—pulling rocks from the soil and piling them on the sledge. Many were so large it took all the strength of both men to move them. When the load filled the sledge, one of them drove the ox to the edge of the field, and they hauled the rocks off and piled them onto the half-finished stone wall.

The drudgery afforded Richard plenty of time to think. Against his will, or so he told himself, his thoughts ran to Sarah with eager feet. He imagined going to Pastor Jewett's house to call on her, and Sarah running to welcome him with a joyful smile and open arms.

He flushed and glanced toward his father. Enough of that! If he let himself muse on such daydreams, his parent would surely guess his unseemly thoughts. It wasn't an impure notion precisely, yet he couldn't shake the feeling that it was an improper one.

Young men were allowed to think about eligible young ladies. But Sarah, though he'd rejoiced to learn she lived, was no longer eligible, at least not in the eyes of his parents. And he must respect his parents, even though he had reached his majority and could think for himself. They were right.

Weren't they?

Sarah lived five years among the heathen.

"So?" his spirit argued as he hefted a stone to the sledge.

So, she has taken on heathen ways.

"Are you sure?"

Decent folk won't receive her.

"The parson and his wife receive her."

But they must.

"How so?" The little voice persisted, and he chose a very large rock that needed all his energy and concentration. Yet when he had strained and groaned and moved it to the sledge, the question remained unanswered, and he could not help arguing with himself again.

They must, because God commands them to love and serve the flock.

"And does not God command you to love the brethren, as well?"

Aye, that He does. But even if I were to overcome the repulsion I feel when I contemplate her experience, I mustn't go against my parents, who are good people.

"And how do you define goodness? Think on the tale of the Good Samaritan. Were not those who passed by the injured man good people, respected in their communities?"

By the end of the day, he was mentally and physically exhausted.

"Come, son," his father called. "It's a good day's work we've done. Let us head for home ere darkness catches us."

Richard plodded to the sledge and dropped one last stone on the load. His father had already unhitched the ox.

"Shan't we unload this tonight?"

"Nay," said his father. " 'Tis only half a load, but twilight falls. We'll come back at first light."

Richard walked wearily beside his father. His shoulder ached where his musket rested on it. Side by side, they shuffled toward home, where a beam of light shone out from the little oiled paper window and through a gap in the palisade.

"Father."

"Yes, son?"

Richard said nothing as they walked toward the gate, knowing that once he broached the subject, he couldn't unsay it.

They paused at the gate, and his father looked at him in the dimness. "What say ye, Richard?"

"I. . .was thinking of Sarah."

His father grunted and opened the gate.

"Is there a reason I should not marry her?"

His father turned slowly and stared at him. Richard felt the unaccountable urge to apologize, but something deep within held him back.

After a long moment of silence, his father said, " 'Twould be a mistake, I fear."

"Why, Father? Her parents are dead. Don't you feel we have sort of an obligation to her?"

"No more than the rest of the town has." His father shook his head. "Best leave it be, son."

"But—"

"Your mother's grief is fresh. She's struggling with the idea that she has to give up on Stephen. He may as well be dead, and she needs to grieve him properly. To bring someone else into the family, someone who has been among the heathen and perhaps learned to sympathize with them. . . Nay, son. Not now. If you've a mind to marry, better to look toward one of the girls who has remained in the community and been faithful at church."

"It wasn't Sarah's fault that she was captured."

"That's so. But think, Richard. She was enslaved by Indians. She may have been compromised. And if not, she has surely embraced some of their savage ways. I know you had notions about her in the old days, and I was not displeased. But things have changed. She is no longer the ideal wife for a God-fearing man."

His father stepped inside the fence and waited for him to enter. Richard stood still. A dark, bleak ache swept over him.

"Son?"

He walked through the gate, and his father closed it firmly.

❧

For two more days, Richard let his father's verdict simmer. On Sunday, his family walked to meeting and sat in their regular pew. Sarah sat in the front with the parson's wife and children and their other two boarders, Miss Hardin and Miss Miller.

From where Richard sat, he could see Sarah, sitting straight and still between the taller Christine Hardin and little Abby Jewett. A streak of sunlight found its way in through the open window, and he thought he caught a faint glint of gold from her hair where it fell below her cap. Not the glorious luster that had gleamed from it of old, but a hint, or better, a promise. Her hair was clean now, though still limp, but the mats and tangles had been combed out. Still, he wouldn't have known her from behind if he hadn't known of her presence in the Jewett household and recognized the fabric Catherine had carried to her a few days past.

All through the reverend's two-hour sermon, his heart warred with his brain. He knew it was sinful, but he couldn't keep his thoughts on what the pastor said. Instead he thought of how thin Sarah's shoulders looked and how she had toughened during her absence. That soft, rounded cast to her face was gone. Her cheeks were gaunt and her eyes sunken.

But that will change, he told himself. A summer in the village with good eating and loving friends, where her labor would be less strenuous than it had been in Canada, would restore her. All she needed was fresh, creamy milk and a good pudding every day, and a kind word or two from one who loved her. If only he could be the one to provide that for her!

When the service ended and they rose, he realized he couldn't tell what the parson had expounded. He sincerely hoped his father didn't quiz him on the sermon. Though he was no longer a child to be chastised, it would still embarrass him.

He lingered, hoping to get a closer view of Sarah, but she stayed at the front with Goody Jewett and the others. She never turned toward them while he watched.

"Come, Richard," his father urged, and he followed his family outside.

A few neighbors spoke to him. He nodded and answered with as few words as possible. He swung around to look back at the doorway, but still Sarah did not appear.

"There be Goodman Fowler and his two daughters," said his mother. She and Catherine went to speak to the young ladies, and his mother threw him a meaningful glance. All too clearly, he saw that she wished him to go and speak to Dorcas and Alice Fowler. In a flash, he knew his father had said something to her about Sarah.

Richard felt betrayed. Although his father had counseled him not to mention Sarah for fear of upsetting his mother, he had gone and done it himself, warned her that Richard had once more turned his attention to the girl he'd admired so long ago. He went to join a cluster of men who discussed cutting an early hay crop and pretended not to notice his mother's glances.

By the time the four headed home at last, he had come to a decision. He would visit the Jewett home on Monday and ask to speak to Sarah. He would ask her what had happened to her since she was removed so cruelly from the village. No more of this speculation. Mother and Father feared she was no longer fit to live among them. Well, he preferred not to pass judgment until he learned the truth. He would ask her straight out what her captivity was like, how she was treated, and if she kept her faith.

❧

A moment's doubt overtook Richard when he raised his hand to knock at the Jewetts' door. For an instant, he considered turning and striding quickly along the path toward home. But as he hesitated, the door flew open. Richard topped the pastor's height by three or four inches, but Jewett stood above him on the floor of the cottage, so he found himself eye to eye with the minister.

Richard caught his breath, stepped backward off the door stone, and nodded. "Morning, Reverend."

"Ah, Richard. May I help you?"

Could he, indeed? Richard cleared his throat and adjusted the musket on his shoulder.

"I. . ." Why on earth hadn't he brought something as an excuse for this visit? He felt the blood rush to his face and hoped his beard covered his discomfiture. "I thought perhaps to have a word with one of your guests."

"Aye?" The pastor relaxed just a hair and smiled. "Which one? All are about the place, I believe. Myself, I'm about to go over to the meetinghouse for some quiet while I study. The children's exuberance makes it difficult here, you understand. But perhaps I should stay?"

"Oh no, sir. Don't discommode yourself. No need at all."

Did a shade of disappointment cross the parson's face? "Well, Miss Hardin and Miss Miller be inside helping my wife—"

"It's Miss Minton I've come to see."

"Ah. The garden, then. She seems to find peace in working the soil. I've warned her to stay within hailing distance of the house and not go to the far corners of our little cornfield without company."

"Aye, sir, I understand you perfectly. Though your house be in the center of the village, we cannot count on safety."

Jewett stepped outside and closed the door. "I'm not wishing to be nosy, Richard, but I stand as a father would to these young ladies now. Might I inquire the purpose of your call?"

"Well, I. . ." The awkward uncertainty assailed Richard once more, coupled with the knowledge that his actions went against his parents' wishes. "I wanted to fully express my condolences to her. We were longtime neighbors and. . .her family and mine. . ."

"Of course. I only ask that you speak to her within full view of the house and any passersby. We mustn't give occasion for gossip when the returned captives hold so fragile a position in the parish. It is my hope to see them reconciled fully into the village in time."

Richard found it difficult to swallow around the painful lump that had risen in his throat. So the parson knew just how deep the mistrust and fear went. He wondered if Jewett knew his parents' intolerance. And his own, when it came to that. Only Catherine had shown a truly magnanimous and forgiving spirit. "Yes, sir."

The pastor eyed him thoughtfully and nodded. "Pray for these ladies, Richard, and the other returned captives, as well. I've visited several of the families who have been reunited with loved ones or taken in orphans. It will take them time to feel comfortable in our society again. Not only those who lived among the savages. Some who lived in the city are finding it hardest. I could tell you about one girl who was a kitchen maid to a wealthy family in Quebec. She had finer clothing and better fare than she has here with her own people."

"Does she wish to go back?" The idea startled Richard.

"Nay, I think not, but she must reconcile her memories and her expectations. Well, then, I'll be on my way. Good day." The pastor nodded and walked up the slope toward the meetinghouse.

Richard rounded the house and spotted Sarah almost immediately, hoeing steadily among the knee-high corn plants. He supposed she didn't mind working in the little cornfield Pastor Jewett had planted that spring. Among the Pennacook, cultivating corn and later grinding the dried kernels into meal must have been among her major duties. But now she hoed good, English soil, with the promise of good company, a filling meal, and a snug berth when the day's toil was done. Was she happy to be here among her own kind? Of course she missed her family. Had she known they were all dead when she left here? Or had she hoped to come home and find them waiting?

And what had she hoped of him?

He walked slowly toward the edge of the corn. No turning back, now that he'd spoken to the parson.

Her slender form bent to the task. She was too intent on her work, he thought. A warrior could sneak up on her easily. But at that moment, she straightened and whirled toward him, and he saw that he was wrong about that. She was not only alert, but instinctive fear had seized her when she sensed his presence.

When she saw him, she ceased her motion for a second and then raised a hand to wipe her brow. Their gazes locked, and she stood immobile.

"Sarah." He spoke her name so softly she couldn't possibly hear it from where she stood, but he saw her lips quiver. She raised the hoe and carefully hiked her skirt just enough to let her pass between the corn plants without disturbing them.

When she reached the edge of the plowed ground, she stopped and rested the hoe blade on the ground. Richard approached one step, then another. About six feet from her, he stopped.

"Good morning." She squinted a little and rocked on her feet, as though she might dash for the house.

He nodded. "I. . ."

The sun glinted off her hair, and for an instant, he saw the old Sarah. The core of her beauty was still there, and it grabbed him so strongly that his stomach lurched.

She took one more step toward him, and he could see the depths of her blue eyes.

"Are you well, Sarah?"

"Aye."

"Be you going to stay here with the Jewetts?"

"For now."

He considered that. Did she have plans? "And then? Will you leave us again?"

"Should I?"

"Nay, but. . ."

"But?" She cocked her head toward her left shoulder and studied him. "The people here treat us differently now than before we were taken away."

"Do we?"

"You know you do."

His mouth went dry. "We don't—that is, I don't mean to."

She said nothing but stared, unmoving, until his guilt spurred him to close the distance between them.

When only two feet of salty New England air separated them, he gathered his courage. "Sarah, I regret how I acted last week."

"Oh?"

"Yes. I. . .couldn't. . ."

"You couldn't bear to look at me and claim me as your friend? You couldn't stand to think that I might have joined the Pennacook in their heathenish ceremonies, is that it? Or perhaps you speculated I'd become worse than a slave to them, I'd thrown away all decency and virtue, I'd—"

"Stop it."

They glared at each other.

Richard couldn't help noticing how alive she looked in that moment. Her cheeks, though still thin, were flushed a becoming pink, and her eyes sparked with passion. He gave a small cough and tried again. "My father—"

"Your father has nothing to do with it, or he shouldn't have! You are a man grown. If you can't own me as your friend—as someone you once cared about—before the whole village, then I won't have you skulking around now apologizing, when none else can see you. I've heard the things people are saying, Richard. If you believe them, you're not the man I thought you were. I thank God I spent the last five years depending on His mercy, not yours."

She turned and walked back into the cornfield, where she wielded the hoe with jerky strokes.

So that's the way you accept an apology. If you think you can cultivate a man's heart the way you do a corn patch, you're mistaken, Sarah Minton.

He hefted his musket and made for the path.

seven

Sarah rued her dismissal of Richard before she reached the end of the row she was hoeing. Of course he was confused and curious. She should not condemn him for taking things slowly in renewing their acquaintance, and he *did* come in private to talk to her, when there were no busybodies listening. Why had she berated him for it? He was trying to sort things out without generating gossip.

She paused and wiped the beads of sweat from her brow. The day had turned quite hot, and her vigorous hoeing, along with her anger, had warmed her. She would stop when she got to the end of the next row, near the house, and go in for a drink of water.

Looking back along the file of young corn plants, she realized what she had just done. Richard had come and said he was sorry, the very thing she had longed to hear since that first painful day when he had ignored her. And she'd sent him away with a blistering rebuke. She wished she had heard him out and explored the depth of his feelings.

He'd said he regretted his actions, and he'd mentioned his father. Had Goodman Dudley led the family in shunning the returned captives? Had he forbidden his children to befriend them?

If such were the case, then she should be grateful that Richard had taken matters into his own hands and come to her, despite his father's feelings. Catherine, too, had shown kindness in bringing her the material for the new clothes she so badly needed. Were the children perhaps more fair-minded than their parents? The Dudleys' younger son, Stephen, was taken captive when Sarah was. Surely the family would not treat him this way should he return to them one day.

Sarah leaned on the hoe, weary to the core. She was tired of always trying to figure out what people thought and how they felt. Why couldn't one be straightforward in dealing with folks? But when she considered that, she wasn't sure she could abide complete honesty among the villagers. If some did not hide their true feelings, their contempt and distrust would show plainly, and chaos would erupt.

A breeze lifted the brim of her bonnet, and she welcomed its relief. It also stirred the leaves of the nearby forest, and she realized how far she was from the pastor's house. She began to chop quickly at the weeds in the next row, working her way steadily back toward the humble parsonage.

❧

The next day it rained, and Sarah spent all morning with Jane, stitching a new dress while Christine continued to weave. Sarah gave Abigail a scrap of the linsey material and a needle so that she could practice her stitches. The three young women had been left with the little girls and their sewing while Elizabeth Jewett joined her husband in calling on several ill parishioners. The two youngest children napped in the loft.

"Mrs. Jewett despairs of finding me a husband," Christine confided to the other two girls when Abby ran outside to the necessary.

"Must they try?" Sarah asked.

Christine shot the shuttle through her web. "It seems the reverend thinks they must. But he fears I'll be harder to unload than you or Jane."

Sarah knew it was true, for she had heard the pastor and his wife discuss Christine's situation during her captivity. The Puritan minister practiced great toleration and charity by harboring one who had lived in a convent. But even with the Reverend Jewett's support, others in the strict community would continue to wonder if Christine had apostatized.

"You gave him your word you've remained faithful," Sarah said.

"Of course. But people have long memories hereabouts."

Jane bit off the end of her thread. "At least you've no foreign marriage to live down. Goody Jewett told me the village gossips' tongues are wagging. I suppose I shouldn't have gone back to my English name. They wonder if I was really married and if Monsieur Robataille is truly dead, or if I just up and walked away from him when Captain Baldwin came on the scene. I thank the Lord I had no babies to bring back with me, as crass as that may sound. These staunch Englishmen wouldn't want to take on a Frenchman's offspring. Look at Madame Bayeux. Her own family didn't want her children. Though I hear they've kept them after all."

Sarah felt heat redden her cheeks. "The truth is, I don't believe I wish to marry."

"Me, either." Christine nodded and ran the shuttle back and forth. "I'd be happy to live as a servant in someone's house, so long as I'm not mistreated."

"Well, I don't know as I'd want to work for someone else all my life," Jane countered.

"That's because you've had your own home," Sarah said. "It must have been good in some ways to be a housewife and run things your own way."

Jane's lips pressed tight together as she bent over her sewing. "I suppose some days were not so bad. But I'll tell you this: A wife without hired help works harder than a servant girl."

A wail came from the corner bed, and Sarah jumped up. "There's Ruth, awake from her nap. I'll get her."

"And I'd best start putting dinner on the table," Jane said. All knew their hosts would return home soon for the meal.

By the time Sarah changed Ruth's clouts, Constance had wakened. Sarah carried Ruth to the bottom of the ladder and watched while the four-year-old descended. Abby came in from outside.

"There, now, girls, you can play with Ruth while we prepare dinner." Sarah set the baby on the quilt that covered the parents' low bed in the corner. Constance obliged by fetching her rag doll and holding it out to Ruth.

As she worked about the hearth with Jane and Christine, Sarah decided she would have another talk with Goody Jewett that evening. She knew the pastor and his wife meant well, and perhaps it would be best for the community if all the young women found husbands. But the idea of being parceled off to a man she hardly knew repelled Sarah. Yes, much better to serve as a hired girl for one of the wealthier families, perhaps at one of the garrison houses.

Richard's image flitted through her mind. Not the Richard from her past, young and optimistic, but the new one—sober, suspicious Richard, who was not ready to trust her even as a friend, let alone as a woman he could love. She doubted he would ever regain the carefree heart he'd had as a lad. He'd seen too much. All of the villagers had. And of course, he'd lost his own brother.

Sarah empathized with Richard and his family. Not knowing your loved ones' fates was perhaps a step worse than seeing them killed. She knew that when the negotiators went to Quebec, Charles Gardner had done his best to get wind of Stephen Dudley's whereabouts, but the Pennacook had closed ranks and kept any whisper of information from him. The Dudleys must be heartbroken.

During her captivity, Sarah had wondered about her own family. Her mother's scream had haunted her, but still, for five years, she had hoped some of her kin might have survived. Captain Baldwin had dispelled those hopes soon after she met him in Quebec City. Both her parents had been cut down by the savages, and her sister, Molly, had apparently died in the fire that leveled their house that night. The captain speculated that Molly was dead before the fire began, but even so, Sarah fought nightmares of her younger sister engulfed in flames.

She shivered and plunked the pewter plates down on the table harder than she'd meant to.

"Are you cold?" Christine asked. "Goody Jewett has a shawl hanging on the peg by the door."

"Nay," Sarah whispered. "Thank you, I'm fine."

But she knew she wasn't ready to go off to live with strangers yet. In just a few days, she had begun to feel secure here with the Jewetts. Until she came back to Cochecho, she'd had hopes of being reunited with her family, though she'd been torn from them in the dark of that awful night and looked back to see flames rising. Still, she had told herself they might have gotten away. As long as she didn't know, it was possible. But since she'd learned their fates, the awful dreams had assailed her.

She would like to stay here awhile, she believed. If the Jewetts would keep her on, she would like to help them with the chores and tending the children until the nightmares stopped.

That evening she found a moment to speak to Goody Jewett, after they'd washed the dishes together, while Christine and Jane put the little girls to bed.

"Of course we want you to stay with us until you're ready, Sarah," the pastor's wife assured her.

"I don't like to be a burden on you." Sarah lowered her gaze, afraid to see rejection in her hostess's eyes.

"Nay, you are a help to me. You've worked in the garden and done the washing. You young ladies are a blessing to me just now." Goody Jewett sneaked a look toward where her husband and the two boys sat at the table, going over the lessons the minister had set for his sons that morning. "You see, we expect another wee one by Christmas. I should be glad if at least one of you stayed with me that long."

Sarah caught her breath. Was this good news? A sixth child coming, and Ruth just beginning to toddle. The parson's family already stretched its resources as far as they could. But Elizabeth smiled at her and squeezed her hand. "My husband hopes for another boy."

Sarah smiled back. "I'm sure that would please him. But. . ."

"But what?" Elizabeth waited for her to speak.

"What if we all three stayed? That would be hard for you. The people won't keep bringing food, will they?"

"We shall see. And I'm sure you girls will find places within a few months' time, whether through marriage or employment."

Sarah wasn't so sure.

❧

Richard set out early for the village to buy provisions for his mother, an empty sack in his hand. Better to get it done and be home before nooning. Then he could put in a full afternoon of work around the farm.

He came within sight of the long, low building, built many

years earlier by Major Waldron. After the major was killed in the massacre, the post was taken over by Joseph Paine. He traded with the Indians but also stocked supplies from the outside world for the settlers.

As Richard drew close, he spotted two figures going into the store: Sarah and one of the other girls boarding at the Jewetts' house. He pulled up short. He almost turned around and went home; however, that would mean another trip to the village, and his mother would scold him for not bringing her the sugar cone and vanilla he had promised to fetch. He ran a hand through his hair and made up his mind. He would only nod to them, unless Sarah initiated a conversation.

As he entered, he noticed a middle-aged couple talking to the trader, apparently haggling over a length of woolen cloth. *Trust Goodman Ackley to squeeze every ha'penny before he let it go.* His wife's sharp tongue would only add to the sport of the trade. Richard thought he would stay away from the trader until the Ackleys were done dealing with him.

Several men stood near the cold hearth, deep in conversation. Richard supposed they chose that spot out of habit—their warm gathering place in the colder months of the year. The two young women had wandered to the far side of the long, low-ceiled room, to where the herbs were stored.

Richard's quest for vanilla beans would take him near them. He paused along the wall where tools hung, eyeing the fox and beaver traps. The two young ladies seemed to have found the item they wanted and stepped away. He drew in a deep breath and walked toward the bench, though he would have to pass close by them.

"Good day." Sarah's soft voice sent a shiver down his spine.

He stopped abruptly between the cinnamon and the lard tubs. "Good day, ladies."

Sarah smiled in the dimness, but the other girl—Jane, was it?—averted her gaze and gave a perfunctory nod.

"How is your mother?" Sarah asked.

"Very well, thank you." He didn't know what else to say and stood there mute for a long moment. Her eyes were gray in this light, but her hair somehow caught a glint from the rays streaming through the window across the room.

Sarah twitched, and he was almost sure her companion had nudged her with a not-too-subtle elbow.

"Pardon us," Sarah said. "We must fill Goody Jewett's list."

"Of course." Richard quickly chose a handful of vanilla beans and carried them to the counter. Trader Paine was still talking to the Ackleys, but he broke away from them and came to tend to Richard's purchase.

"Will that be all?"

"Nay, my mother requests a cone of white sugar if you've any on hand." Richard slid a coin toward the trader.

"Indeed I do." Paine bent beneath his rough worktable and lifted a heavy object wrapped in paper and set it on the surface.

Richard opened his sack, and Paine lifted the sugar cone. As they worked together to fit the unwieldy object into the bag, Richard heard Goody Ackley, who stood three feet from him, mutter something about "those shameless girls the parson took in."

Richard turned and stared at the woman. How dare she say such things about Sarah and her companion? But sure enough, she was eyeing the two young women across the store with a contemptuous sneer on her lips.

"I beg your pardon, ma'am?" Richard said in a voice loud enough that the men at the hearth broke off their words and looked toward him.

"Nothing," said Goody Ackley, glancing toward her husband.

"Strange," Richard replied, his anger taking hold and spurring him to speak when ordinarily he would have kept silent. "I thought I heard you comment on the parson's houseguests."

"Oh, it's strange, all right." The goodwife wrinkled her nose, and her eyes nearly closed as she flicked a glance toward the two distant figures. "Strange that our minister would harbor fallen women in his household."

Richard felt heat surge through his body. "That is vile language. You ought to be in the stocks for speaking such base things about women who were carried off against their wills and have shown only meekness since their return."

"Here!" Goodman Ackley stepped between Richard and his wife and glared up at the tall young man. "Don't you speak to my wife like that. The idea of a churchgoing man defending a jade who's lived years with a French trapper!"

Before he gave any thought to his actions, Richard pulled back his fist and smacked the man's jaw.

eight

Ackley fell backward and tumbled to the floor.

His wife gasped and knelt over her husband.

Richard winced and rubbed his knuckles.

"You—you—you wild young jackanapes," Goody Ackley sputtered at him. "I'll have the constable on you!"

"Nay," the trader said calmly, throwing Richard a weary smile. " 'Tis you and your husband who should fear the law, ma'am. Dudley is right about that. Folk are put in the stocks for far milder slander than the two of you have uttered here this day."

Richard nodded gravely at Paine, picked up his sack, and turned to go. To his dismay, he saw that every eye in the trading post was on him, including those of Sarah. Jane Miller's face was scarlet, and Sarah's a stark white. For a moment, no one moved. Then Sarah slipped the item that she'd held onto the nearest shelf, and the two young women headed silently for the door.

Richard looked at the trader, and Paine returned his gaze with a resigned look. All Richard could gather from it was Paine's support, but regret that the incident had occurred in his place of business. Even though he disliked the Ackleys, Paine would have to trade with them in the future, just as he traded with the nearby Indians nobody trusted.

Richard nodded and walked out. Outside the door, he stopped in surprise.

Sarah and her companion huddled together under the

eaves, and Sarah stepped forward as he emerged. "Richard, thank you. I hope you are not hurt."

"Nay, it was nothing." He looked past her and saw that Jane stood apart with hunched shoulders. Tears trickled down her cheeks.

"Allow me to see you ladies home," Richard said.

"We'll be fine," Sarah assured him. "But I needed to thank you for taking our part. You didn't have to."

"I know." He shrugged. "They spoke nasty lies. I probably overstepped the bounds of propriety, but I didn't feel I should let it go."

Jane looked him in the face for the first time. "Sir, you don't know how often people speak such things. You can't be about to silence them every time."

"Nay, but if one man speaks up one time and others hear, perhaps the next time the others will take your part."

Sarah reached out to squeeze his arm. "You speak truth."

"Come." He hefted his sack, wincing at the stab of pain in his knuckles, and started along the path toward the parsonage. They walked without speaking, with Sarah between him and Jane. When they reached the parson's dooryard, he smiled ruefully at them. "Perhaps Goody Jewett will go with you next time, though young ladies ought to be able to do a bit of trading without fear."

"Yes." The troubled frown between Sarah's eyebrows accentuated her thin face. She wasn't fully recovered yet from her ordeal, he realized, but she was beginning to regain the weight she had lost. No longer did her features bear that emaciated look.

Richard's pulse quickened as he surveyed her. In another month, she would have regained her beauty, he was sure. He cleared his throat. "Would you like me to go back and fetch

Goody Jewett's needs for you?"

Sarah shook her head. "Thank you, but nay. I shall tell the reverend what happened today, and I expect he shall want to settle this matter himself."

❧

She watched Richard leave, striding down the path with long, confident steps. He had done what she'd longed for the day she returned, and now she was in turmoil.

True, he had defended Jane and Christine, as well as her— mostly Jane—and he probably would have done so had she not been present. Instead of disheartening her, that raised her appreciation of his action even more.

This was the Richard she'd kept alive in her heart for five years. This was a man who stood for truth and protected the poor and downtrodden. She had not been mistaken all this time. Richard had grown into the man she had dreamed of loving.

As she pondered this, she had no hope, in spite of her fierce attraction to him. Richard didn't want to marry her. The townspeople looked down on her now. Even if he had wanted to marry her, she couldn't saddle him with that burden.

She turned toward the door, certain that the right course for her would be to remain single and serve God however she could.

Jane stood waiting for her on the door stone, watching her keenly. She raised her chin. "He's a good man. He put himself in danger of censure for us."

"Aye." Sarah went in with her, and when Goody Jewett heard her tale, she left the children in care of Christine and Jane.

"You and I will go straight to Samuel," Elizabeth Jewett declared, taking off her apron.

Sarah walked behind her to the meetinghouse and waited meekly outside while Elizabeth went inside to tell her husband what had happened at the trading post.

The Reverend Jewett came to the door and looked out at her, his blue eyes filled with concern. "Are you and Miss Miller all right, Miss Minton?"

"Yes, sir," Sarah replied. "Jane was mortified, but Richard Dudley's actions will be put about the community ere nightfall, I'm sure."

"Oh, I've no doubt," the pastor agreed wryly. He looked toward the river, where the trading post lay. "I expect I should go have a word with Goodman Ackley, and also with the trader." He leaned against the doorjamb, and Elizabeth peeked out beside him.

"Think ye the constable should be notified?" his wife asked.

"Not by us. Richard and Paine heard what was said. They can lodge a complaint of gossip if they wish."

"What if. . ." Sarah gulped and looked up at them. "What if Goodman Ackley sues Richard?"

Pastor Jewett shook his head. "If he's determined to do that, he can, but it seems to me he'd have no case. Most people will sympathize with Richard."

"Are you sure?" Sarah asked. The majority of the community still seemed to look on the former captives with distaste.

The parson slid his arm around his wife and pulled her against his side.

Sarah pretended not to notice. Such a display of affection was seldom made in public, and she doubted Reverend Jewett was conscious of his act as he spoke to her.

"I'm sorry you young ladies have seen the cruel side of the sinful nature. I'll speak to Goodman Ackley and his wife. It may not do any good, but it's part of my job to keep peace in the parish. If they won't listen. . ."

"I wouldn't expect a quick apology," Elizabeth said, and her husband frowned.

"Well, I'd best get over to their house." He dropped his arm to his side and walked down the steps of the meetinghouse.

"When you speak to Mr. Paine, would you bring me the candlewicking and pepper Sarah and Jane went for, if it's not too much trouble?" Elizabeth asked.

"Surely. And afterward, I shall come back here to finish planning my Sunday sermon." He looked up at the blue sky. "Odd. It's on forgiveness."

⁂

As the long summer days passed, Richard threw himself into the work of the farm, often toiling at his father's side from first light to sunset. During his hours of steady labor, Sarah's face often flitted through his mind.

But more and more, another haunted him—Stephen.

His brother's capture angered him. The negotiators who redeemed the captives had done all they could and spent every penny they had but found no word of Stephen.

As time passed, Richard saw his parents, especially his mother, grow old before his eyes. Her hair whitened, and her step slowed. Catherine seemed to be taking on more of the housework, and their mother spent more time in her chair, knitting or simply sitting with her hands folded in her lap. She spoke little and smiled less. Richard knew she grieved for Stephen, perhaps more heavily than when he first left them.

When the corn stood nearly to his waist, Richard and his father turned to haying. In order to keep livestock through the long, harsh winter of New Hampshire, they needed to stockpile hay, corn, and cornstalks to feed the cattle, sheep, and chickens. In winter, when they cut trees to dry for the next year's firewood, they always cut in a pattern that would open up new fields for them to grow hay. The number of livestock they could keep depended on the winter feed they could produce.

Richard eyed the gardens and the hayfields often, counting off the days until he might leave his father for a while. Goodman Dudley still had his strength, though he also showed his age in swatches of gray hair at his temples. But to provide for four adults and gradually improve their life, he needed the help of his grown son.

In mid-July, after the first cutting of hay was safely stacked, Richard dared broach the subject. As they were milking one evening, he took his wooden bucket of milk and went to where his father was finishing with the second cow. "I want to go to Canada, Father."

His father's hands paused in the rhythmic motion of milking then went on.

"It is too dangerous."

"Charles said he and Baldwin's crew were received well enough when they went."

"They had the governor's backing. What could you do that those men did not do, son?"

"I don't know, but if I don't try, I will always wonder."

His father sighed and stood up, lifting his milking stool and bucket. "I can't let you go, Richard. Imagine how your mother would take it if anything happened to you."

Richard turned away disappointed. *I will wait until after the harvest*, he told himself.

A fortnight later, he gathered his courage, and on a quiet evening, he left his parents' home and walked once more to the parsonage.

&

After supper, Pastor Jewett took all the children but Ruth for a walk to the river so they could enjoy the evening breeze that came up from the sea, tempering the heat of the July day.

Goody Jewett sat in her chair by the open doorway, lulling Ruth to sleep, while Sarah, Jane, and Christine made short work of cleaning up the kitchen.

As Sarah hung her damp linen towel on a peg to dry and Christine set the last pewter mug on the shelf, Mrs. Jewett called out to an approaching visitor, "Good evening, sir, and welcome."

A deep voice replied, "Good even to you, ma'am."

Sarah felt a shiver of anticipation as she recognized Richard's voice. For the past month, she had seen him only at Sunday meeting. He sometimes spoke to her briefly, no more than a "Good day." His sister was more vocal, often stopping to chat with her and the other young women. But sometimes as Sarah left the meetinghouse with Goody Jewett and the children, she would see Richard gazing at her from across the yard, and she often wondered where his thoughts led.

"Be Sarah Minton about?"

Her heart leaped at his quiet inquiry, and she fumbled with the strings of her apron.

"Let me help you," Jane hissed, pushing her around and seizing the ties.

"Why yes," Goody Jewett said, shifting in her chair so she could call into the room. "Sarah? A visitor has come a-calling."

Sarah pulled in a deep breath and stared at Jane. She'd told the other girls she didn't wish to marry, and yet a glorious hope dawned in her heart when she realized Richard had come all the way into town to see her.

Jane smiled and squeezed her arm. "Best see what he wants."

Sarah's knees trembled as she walked slowly toward the door. The setting sun streaked the clouds behind Richard with pink, mauve, and scarlet, but the display could not rival the burst of joy inside her.

"Welcome, Richard." She ducked her head, conscious of the eyes watching her.

His smile was contained and nervous. "I. . .wondered if we might walk. With Goody Jewett's consent, of course."

Mrs. Jewett smiled. "You may, provided you stay within sight of this house, sir." She struggled to stand without disturbing the sleeping little girl in her arms.

Sarah reached to take Ruth from her. "Let me take her to the loft."

Goody Jewett drew back. "Nay, I think Christine is waiting just behind you to do that task for me. Your guest awaits." She smiled gently, and Sarah let her arms fall to her sides.

"Aye." She glanced again at Richard. He had retreated a few steps and stood waiting for her.

"Come in before full dark," Mrs. Jewett murmured as she passed her, and Sarah nodded.

Delicious coolness bathed her as she stepped outside. Richard met her gaze then looked down at the toes of his boots. "Perhaps we could stroll along the near edge of the fields?"

"Certainly." She walked beside him around the house and to the border of the corn that now reached her waist.

Richard looked out over the rows and pulled in a deep breath. "Parson looks to make a good crop this year."

"Yes, we've had fine weather. Enough rain, but hot days for growing." She felt a bit silly, discussing weather and crops with a grown man. But that might be better than addressing the real reason Richard had come. Her pulse throbbed faster, and she stared straight ahead as she walked.

"I've been thinking about Stephen a lot these days," he confessed as they reached the end of Pastor Jewett's field and moved on to the edge of Goodman Bryce's. "Charles Gardner tells me he's likely been adopted by an Indian family and is happy there. What think ye?"

Sarah's giddy feelings fled as the memories of her own Indian family and the lean years in the Pennacook village returned. She had imagined that Richard came with thoughts of courting, but instead he only sought her out for her knowledge of the Indians. Still, it was better than being shunned, and perhaps they could restore their old friendship over time.

"Charles is probably correct. When he came to my village to redeem me, my people—that is, the family who adopted me—hid me at first. But after they had talked a long time, they brought me out and handed me over to the white men. I was overcome with joy and fear and disbelief. Charles asked me right away about Stephen, and I told him all I knew, which was little."

"You'd seen Stephen in Canada?"

"We were in the same group when we were taken, but they split into smaller bands before we came to the village where I lived most of the time. The warriors who took Stephen went off westward—toward Montreal, I supposed—but I had no real idea where they'd taken him. I did see Stephen one more time, about two years later. His people came through where we lived and stopped with us a few days."

Richard stopped walking and stared at her. "I didn't know this. Were you able to speak to him?"

"I tried." She looked back toward the houses of the village. "I saw a chance the second day, when he was out with some of our boys, practicing throwing knives. I pretended to be working, but I moved closer until he looked up and saw me. I said his name. *Stephen.* He looked at me as if I'd spoken in Greek. And he turned and walked away. I was going to follow him, hoping he would acknowledge me when he was away from the others, but my. . .mother—the woman who. . ." She glanced up at Richard in confusion. Would he understand, or would he think her disloyal to her own family?

He arched his eyebrows. "Your Indian mother?"

"Yes. She came up behind me and seized my arm. She dragged me into her lodge and wouldn't let me go out again until the visitors were gone. I ground corn and worked hides, all the while praying for another chance." The memory of the painful bruise on her forearm made Sarah wince, and she rubbed the spot, although it had long ago healed. "I never saw him again. I'm sorry, Richard."

"It's not your fault."

"Perhaps. But if I'd bided my time and been discreet. . . Oh, I'm so sorry I can't give you better news." Tears flooded her eyes, and she wished she'd kept her apron to wipe them with. She raised her arm and swiped at them with her sleeve.

"Shh."

Richard touched her shoulder, and that made her sob. She wasn't sure whether the tears were for Stephen, or for Richard and his family, or for herself.

"He's probably not unhappy," she ventured.

"Aye. I fear you are right." Richard frowned, and she wished she could unsay the words.

"It's better than. . ." She stopped. Was it really better than what had happened to Molly? Would she rather know Molly lived contentedly among the savages than that she had died in the slaughter that bloody night? Seeing the crosses in the churchyard with her parents' and sister's names carved on them had brought it home to her a few weeks ago. Molly was at rest. But Stephen roamed with the warriors. Perhaps he would even take part in raids against English settlers.

In Richard's face, she saw the same turmoil she was feeling.

"I want to try to find him," he said.

"No, Richard. Don't go. It will only bring you deeper grief."

"Don't you see? While I do nothing, I feel as though I've betrayed my family and my faith. I can't let my brother go wild and heathen without trying my best to stop it. I can't, Sarah."

She drew a shaky breath and reached out to him.

Richard took her hand for a moment and held it in his strong, warm one. "I'm glad you at least had people who didn't mistreat you too badly."

She nodded. "It was difficult. They live in extreme poverty most of the time, but they know no other way. When they have a good harvest or a successful hunt, they do put food away for the lean times. But it always runs out during the winter." She shivered. "As you say, I had it better than some. I worked hard. I learned new skills. And I tried to be the daughter my new mother craved."

"They had no children of their own?"

"Oh, yes. She had three grown sons. Her husband died before I came there. And she'd had a little daughter years ago who grew to about the age I was when I went there. I think that is why they chose to keep me. She wanted a girl to replace her daughter who had died. I was the right size, and I suppose I seemed docile but strong and healthy. I later learned that the man who had captured me and took me to her was one of her sons. When I could speak their language well enough, she told me she had asked him to bring her a daughter to comfort and serve her in her old age, as his sister would have done."

Richard looked down at her with troubled brown eyes. "They give no thought to the mothers grieving here for the children they've lost."

"It is true." She looked around and noticed that the sun had dropped below the dark evergreens. "We must return," she said.

"Aye. Thank you, Sarah."

They walked back toward the parsonage, and although one more bit of information surfaced in Sarah's mind, she wasn't sure whether or not to tell him.

As they approached the house, he paused for a moment. "I plan to go," he said earnestly. "Sarah, if you go to meeting one Sunday and I'm not there, you'll know I've gone to seek Stephen."

"I wish you wouldn't. You will not find him."

He only clamped his lips together and gazed off into the distance.

Sarah sighed. "If you do go. . ."

"Yes?"

"I can tell you the names of the family that adopted Stephen. I learned them after they took him away again. I asked other young women in our village, and they told me the names. And your brother's new name."

"Charles told me nothing of this."

"He probably did not want to cause you more sorrow."

"But you told him when you first saw him in Canada this spring?"

"Yes. It made him hopeful that he could succeed in his

mission, but not so." She eyed him with sadness, fearing she had only made things worse for him. "Charles knew the land, the people, the language, and he still could not find your brother."

"I know." Richard took a deep breath. "You will write down the names for me?"

"If you wish it."

"Thank you. I will find Stephen."

Sarah's heart ached. Richard had no idea how rigorous the journey would be or the discouragement that awaited him. He refused to consider the danger he would encounter. Had she just destroyed her only chance of a happy future?

nine

A fortnight later, as soon as the morning dew evaporated, Sarah and Christine went out to gather petals from the blossoms lading the rosebush at the corner of the parsonage. Christine had learned at the convent how to distill rosewater in a Dutch oven, and she had promised to make some for the pastor's wife to use in her baking.

"It's a pity to ruin all the flowers," Sarah said as she held a stem carefully between its thorns and stripped off the pink petals.

Christine held the basket beneath Sarah's hands to catch the colorful bits as they fluttered down. "We won't need all of the roses. Let's save a few of the best blooms and take them to Goody Jewett." She glanced up and nodded toward the village street. "Yon comes your beau and his friend."

Sarah looked over her shoulder and saw Richard Dudley and Charles Gardner approaching them. Her mouth went dry, but when she glanced at Christine, she realized her friend was even more uncomfortable.

"I'll take this inside," Christine murmured.

"Nay, stay here," Sarah said. Richard and Charles had left the street, and by now it was obvious they intended to converse with the two young women.

"Good day, ladies," Richard said, doffing his hat.

Christine lowered her gaze and nodded.

"Good day, Richard," Sarah said. "Mr. Gardner."

Charles pulled his hat off and stood, holding it and looking at the ground. Sarah took in their appearance. Both held muskets and carried full packs on their backs.

"Charles and I are heading to Quebec," Richard said. "He will take me to the village where he redeemed you, and we will begin our inquiries there."

At a loss for words, Sarah looked into the depths of his eyes, rich brown shot through with gold. She sensed a challenge in them, and the set to his chin told her that nothing she could say would deter him. She looked to Charles instead. "Mr. Gardner, can't you dissuade him from this quest?"

"I'm afraid not, ma'am. And if he must go, then he must."

She turned back to Richard. "You've asked your friend to tread again the fruitless paths he trod a few months ago?"

"Nay, Charles is the one who suggested I might like a companion."

Charles nodded decisively, though his frown showed his disapproval. "I should hate to see my dearest friend undertake this unhappy mission alone, and so I've determined to go with him. At least I can translate for him among some of the tribes, and as you say, I've walked these paths before and can guide Richard. We will travel speedily, the two of us. We hope to be back before snowfall."

"But, Richard, I thought you were going to wait until your father had his harvest in."

"I cannot do that and hope to make this journey before winter. Father has agreed to trade work with some of the other men in my absence."

With early August upon them, Sarah realized they had only three or four months of good traveling weather ahead, and it would take all of that for them to go on foot into the northern wilderness, make their inquiries, and return.

"So. . .you are going now? Today?"

"Aye." Richard gazed at her and took an uncertain step forward, standing just inches from her. "We spoke to Parson Jewett ere we came here. He promises to uphold us in prayer. Will you do the same, Sarah?"

"Of course." A great sadness swept over her. She wanted to reach out to him, to embrace him and plead with him not to go, but that would be useless and most indecorous. "If you get to where I lived, you might have better success if you take a gift."

"We've a few trade goods, but we cannot carry much." He glanced toward Charles.

"I picked up a few knives and some tobacco at the trading post," Charles said.

She nodded. "You might learn something from the women, too. When I was captured, the warriors stole many trinkets and household goods, but the old woman who adopted me was most pleased by. . ." She paused as a lump rose in her throat and tears pricked her eyes at the memory. "Her son brought her some English clothes. They like to get them. Her favorite thing was a bright apron pieced from scraps of red and green cloth. I thought. . ." The tears filled her eyes, and she took a deep breath then went on. "I thought it was one made by Goody Waldron, and old Naticook used to wear it hung about her shoulders like a shawl. It made me laugh to see her wear it that way, but. . .it made me cry, as well."

Charles said, "If we had more men, or a pack animal. . ."

Sarah nodded and reached into the pocket tied about her waist. "Here. This is small." She pulled out a square of soft, fine linen on the corners of which she had stitched bunches of roses. "Take it. If you come to my village, ask for Naticook. Give her this and tell her I am happy with my people. Perhaps she will tell you where Stephen's band lives."

Charles accepted the handkerchief and tucked it into his vest. "Thank you."

Christine stirred. "If you can carry more—"

"I think not, but thank you, ma'am," Charles said.

Christine ducked her head and reverted to silence once more, staring down at the ground.

"Your parents. . . ," Sarah ventured.

Richard frowned. "They are not happy about my decision, but Father understands that I must do this."

She looked long into his eyes and again saw his resolve and a plea for approval. Regardless of those watching, she reached out and touched his sleeve.

"God speed you, Richard."

"Farewell, then." He nodded briskly and gave a quick glance that included Christine. Then he and Charles turned and walked back to the village street and turned west, the way Sarah and the others had come into the town nearly three months ago.

"His family wished him not to go," Christine said.

"So it seems. And I can't blame them. They've lost one son, and the journey Richard is undertaking is a dangerous one." Sarah watched until the two young men disappeared from sight.

"And yet they long as much as he does for any scrap of news."

"Yes, I'm sure that's why his father let him go."

"He's a grown man," Christine said. "Surely they couldn't stop him."

"Nay, but Richard would not defy his father." Sarah sighed and looked at the fragrant basket of rose petals Christine still held in her hands. "Have we enough now? Let us go and make our concoction. Perhaps I can go over to the Dudleys' one day and help his mother and sister put up food for the winter. I can even work in the hayfields if they'll let me."

"Goodman Dudley would never allow you to work out in the fields all day."

"I did it in the Indian village on many occasions, hoeing corn from dawn to dusk."

"Still. . .Parson and Goody Jewett let you tend their garden, but they won't have you stay out there all day in the hot sun."

"True," Sarah said as they walked toward the house. "Elizabeth is very kind. She always insists I wear a bonnet and come inside frequently to rest and refresh myself. Life at the parsonage is far different from the Pennacook village."

She thought of her life there, where Naticook saw her fed and clothed but never expressed concern or affection, requiring instead constant work. Here the arduous work seemed pleasant, and the expectation that she would spend the next winter with the boisterous Jewett family in a snug little house with plenty of firewood stacked outside made the future pleasant to contemplate, rather than frightening as she'd found it during her captivity.

"His family will miss Richard sorely, though," Christine said.

"Aye. In a few days, I will ask permission to visit Goody Dudley and Catherine."

"I'll go with you. Perhaps I can do some mending or spinning for the goodwife."

Sarah smiled at her friend, knowing Christine would not have made the offer if she wasn't sure they would find only women in the house when they paid their call. After her years in the convent, Christine was not used to men and still cringed when they were around, though she seemed to be getting used to the parson's booming voice and energetic presence in the Jewett household. She seldom walked in the village and always hung back with the children on Sunday, as though she hoped no one would speak to her. Sarah thought Christine quite lovely with her tall, willowy form and grace of movement, but Christine seemed unconscious of that and wanted only peace and solitude. Sometimes Sarah wondered if Christine would ever be happy, or if she would live out a fearful, lonely life at the loom.

"Mayhap we'll get enough rosewater today that we can take Richard's mother some," Sarah suggested.

Christine smiled a tiny, timid smile. "I think the gentleman has plans for when he returns."

"If they find Stephen, you mean?" Sarah asked.

"Regardless of whether they find him or nay. He looks like a man of a mind to court."

Sarah felt the blood rush to her cheeks. "Come, we have much to do."

❧

Sarah's opportunity to visit the Dudleys came sooner than she had expected. Only three days after Richard's departure, Catherine Dudley arrived panting on the Jewetts' door stone at noon, while the family sat at dinner.

"Pastor, come," Catherine gasped. "We need you."

The Reverend Jewett jumped up from his stool at the table. "What is it?"

"My father. He dropped a tree on himself this morn. My mother found him when he did not answer the call for dinner."

"Shall I come?" Elizabeth Jewett asked.

"I'll go," Sarah said quickly. Goody Jewett's pregnancy had begun to show, and Sarah knew she often felt nauseous in the morning and fatigued easily.

"How bad is it?" the pastor asked. The minister was indeed called on often when accidents occurred, though for nursing of the sick, Goody Baldwin was often summoned. The captain's wife was known for her skill at midwifery, and between her and the Reverend Jewett, the people of the parish got by without a trained physician.

Catherine leaned against the doorjamb. "He surely has broken a leg and perhaps done other damage to his innards."

Elizabeth got up and hurried to her. "Sit down, child. Rest a moment while my husband and Sarah gather some rags for bandages."

"Mother has his worst wounds bound up." Catherine took a seat and accepted the dipper of water Jane silently offered.

"Has your mother any willow bark?" Elizabeth asked.

"I don't know. We got him to the house with the ox cart, and she told me to hurry to bring Pastor. I didn't stop to see all that she would do for Father."

While they spoke, Sarah dashed about and grabbed a basket and her shawl. Christine, Jane, and Elizabeth tossed several items into the basket, including the fever-reducing willow bark, a few rags, and a bowl holding half the blueberries the children had picked that morning.

The parson didn't own a musket, but he carried a sturdy walking stick whenever he went about the village. He fetched it and reached to take the basket from Sarah. "Are you ready, ladies? Ben, you come with us, and you can run back to give your mother the news after I've looked at Goodman Dudley. Let us not delay any further."

He stepped outside, and Sarah and Catherine followed. Ben trotted ahead, and the other three walked along together until the path narrowed at the edge of the village proper. Then the pastor took the lead, and the two girls walked behind him.

He kept up a moderate pace so that they wouldn't tire, and soon they were within sight of the Dudleys' palisade. Ben had outdistanced them by a few yards, but he waited for them outside the tall fence.

Catherine had left the gate open in her haste, and they entered the compound and stepped up to the house. Catherine hastened in ahead of Sarah and the reverend to announce their arrival.

"Oh, Pastor, I'm so glad you've come," Goody Dudley cried. "There's no one better than you to pray over folks and set bones."

"How is he?" Catherine asked, searching her mother's face.

"Much the same as when you left," Goody Dudley replied.

"Let me see the patient," the pastor said as he leaned his staff in the corner.

Sarah waited with Catherine in the kitchen, and Ben sat down on the doorstep. The Dudleys' home was divided into two rooms on the lower level, with a bedchamber boarded off beneath the loft. From within the chamber, Sarah heard Catherine's father murmur a greeting to the Reverend Jewett. Moments later, his moans reached her ears.

Catherine jumped up and grabbed the iron kettle that sat on the hearth. "We must fetch some water. There will be much washing to do."

Sarah picked up an empty bucket and followed her outside.

"Ben, you may help us," Catherine told the boy. "Have you a well at the parsonage?"

"Nay. We draw our water from the river."

"Well, we have a nice dug well, and you may lower the bucket and haul it up again and fill our vessels for us. Sarah and I shall carry the water into the house."

This kept them bustling for several minutes, and they had

just finished filling every pot and pail available, and even a washtub, when Goody Dudley came from the inner chamber.

"How is Father?" Catherine asked.

"The parson needs help in setting the leg, and it is still bleeding some."

"Can we help him do it?"

"Nay," said her mother. "He advised me to send young Ben to the nearest neighbor." She went to the door and instructed Ben on the errand. "After you tell him to come, your father says you are to go on home and tell your mother the parson will be home ere nightfall."

"Aye, ma'am, I'll have Goodman Ackley here in a trice," Ben promised. He tore out through the gate and down the path toward the village.

Goody Dudley turned back into the house. "What good girls you are. Just look at all the water you've hauled." Her eyes focused on Sarah for the first time. "Thank you for coming."

Sarah nodded. "I thought perhaps you'd need help after the pastor leaves. I could do chores while you sit with your husband, ma'am."

Catherine squeezed her arm. "How kind of you! Shall you sleep here tonight? I've been lonesome since Richard left, and there's no one on the other side of the wall at night."

Sarah glanced up at the loft, where a rough partition separated the two sleeping areas. "If your mother has no objection, I should be happy to." She threw a guarded glance at Goody Dudley.

Her hostess hesitated only a moment. "I'm sure Catherine would find your presence a comfort."

"It would comfort me exceedingly," Catherine agreed. "But, Mother, does the parson think Father will mend all right?"

"He says it will take time. It's a bad break, and Father's

midsection is bruised severely. Some ribs may be broken. After the leg is set, the parson will wrap his middle. He will need to rest for several weeks, I'm sure."

"Oh, Mother!" Catherine flung herself into Goody Dudley's arms and sobbed. "Why did this have to happen with Richard gone?"

"There, now." Her mother rubbed Catherine's back. "I'm sure the Almighty has His purpose in this, though I've not had time to consider what that might be."

"Perhaps the parson can tell us." Catherine pulled back and sniffed. "What shall Sarah and I do now, Mother? I was going to pick beans today, but. . ."

"Why should you not?" her mother asked. "Reverend Jewett will probably be some time attending to your father. I expect he will want you girls out of the house while he and Goodman Ackley set Father's leg. Now, I must gather some linen for him to use to wrap his ribs with."

Sarah gave her the rags Goody Jewett had sent. She was glad for a reason to be outside when Goodman Ackley arrived. She had not forgotten his cruel remark about Jane, though weeks had passed since the incident at the trading post.

"Come, Catherine," she said. "Let's get the beans and cook some for supper."

"But the washing. . ."

"We shall do that later," Sarah assured her.

Goody Dudley nodded. "Yes, after the doctoring is done, I shall gather up all the soiled bedding and clothing to be washed."

As she and Catherine headed out to the kitchen garden, Sarah saw Goodman Ackley puffing up the path toward the house.

"Let's see who can fill her basket first," Sarah said.

Catherine entered into the game and dashed to the rows of beans, swinging her gathering basket.

A few minutes later, both containers were filled to the brim. Sarah wished they hadn't picked so fast, for now they had no excuse to stay outside. "If we had a pot, we could snap the beans out here in the shade," she suggested.

Catherine frowned. "We filled all the pots with water, remember? But mayhap we can dump out my basket and use it for the snapped beans."

They sat down on the grass and set to work, breaking off the ends and snapping the pods with their fingers, filling Catherine's basket with short lengths of green beans.

"I know Charlie Gardner would come help with our field work if he hadn't gone with Richard." Catherine sighed and reached for a handful of beans from Sarah's basket.

"Your other neighbors will help," Sarah assured her.

"Oh, I know it, but everyone is busy this time of year. Mother will hate to ask them."

"Don't fret about it. The parson will likely set up a time for different ones to come. That's what they did when Isaiah Pottle was injured. And perhaps he'll let Ben come stay during harvest. He could be a big help."

"Well, they won't be harvesting the corn or the oats for a while yet," Catherine said. "I can feed the livestock and milk and gather the eggs. I do a lot of that anyway."

"And I will stay as long as you wish and help you with those things and with the cooking and the washing. . .whatever you and your mother need done."

Catherine reached to squeeze Sarah's hand. "Your coming is a blessing. I was very frightened when I saw how badly hurt Father was. I'd been moping around for days anyway, since

Richard went. But now—oh, I know it will be hard for Father to rest, and I wish he wouldn't have such pain, but I'm glad you're here. I haven't had a girl stay at the house for ages."

Sarah smiled at her. "I'll enjoy my visit."

When they entered cautiously, bearing their baskets of snapped beans, the Reverend Jewett and Goodman Ackley were seated near the hearth sipping mugs of tea.

"Ah, young ladies! I see that your hands have not been idle." The pastor stood and bowed to them.

Goodman Ackley climbed awkwardly to his feet and ducked his head without meeting their eyes.

"How is Father?" Catherine asked.

The pastor winced. "He's resting now. Your mother is sitting with him. I'm sure he'll recover from this, but I've suggested your mother get Goody Baldwin to help her with the nursing. Of course, if Sarah wishes to stay a few days. . ."

"I should like to, sir," Sarah said, "though I'm not a skilled nurse."

"And I should like it, as well." Catherine smiled at her, and Sarah felt warmth spread through her, although Goodman Ackley still avoided looking at her.

"I must be going," Ackley said.

"Thank you for helping," said the parson.

Ackley gave a brief nod. "I'll come back to help cut Dudley's next hay crop, after I get mine done."

"That's most kind of you," Catherine said.

Ackley clapped on his hat and went out.

"Well, then," said Catherine, "I suppose we should start thinking about supper, Sarah. I wonder if Father will want to eat?"

"I recommend a light broth tonight." The pastor picked up his hat from the table and reached for his walking stick.

"I shall head for home. Sarah, will you need anything brought to you for your stay?"

Sarah shot a glance at Catherine, who stepped forward with confidence.

"Oh, don't you worry about Sarah, Pastor. We shall take good care of her, and if she has need of clothing and such, she can borrow from me. I think we're nearly of a size."

Pastor Jewett nodded. "So be it. Tell your mother I shall stop in after dinner tomorrow and that if she needs anything before then, she should send you. But you girls must stay together if you come into the village."

"We will," Sarah promised. No one mentioned Catherine's solitary dash to the village to fetch the parson earlier. Everyone knew that utmost caution was needed since the Indians had begun their raids several years earlier, but in dire circumstances, one did what one had to do.

The girls worked quietly about the kitchen, and an hour later, Catherine's mother emerged from the bedchamber with an armload of crumpled linens.

"Father is sleeping," she told them.

Catherine's face paled at the sight of the bloodstained clothing and sheets, but she said only, "Sarah and I can wash those things up before supper, can't we, Sarah?"

"Yes, indeed. We've a tub of cold water waiting outside." Sarah took the bundle from her hostess and headed for the door, knowing the blood would wash out easier in cold water than in hot.

She and Catherine spent the better part of an hour doing laundry; then they went in to find that Goody Dudley had started baking a batch of corn pone on the hearth and put the beans and a bit of salt pork over the coals to simmer. The girls had picked a head of cabbage, and Sarah set about chopping it while Catherine set the table.

"The pork broth is for Father, I suppose," Catherine said. "Our meat supply is getting low again, and I see Mother only put a small piece on to cook."

"It will flavor our beans nicely," Sarah said.

She liked working with Catherine. The Dudleys' large kitchen seemed spacious and airy compared to the Jewetts' crowded house. It reminded her of the old days, when she and Molly helped their mother in the little house by the river.

At dusk, Sarah peeked into the bedchamber to tell Goody Dudley that the broth was ready. Catherine's father lay stretched out on the rope bed, his injured leg propped up with pillows. He seemed to be dozing.

Goody Dudley rose and took the bowl from Sarah. "He's restless," she said. "Sometimes he tries to toss about. I think that leg pains him a great deal."

"Shall we start some more willow bark tea?" Sarah asked.

"Aye. And I believe I'll have you girls help me fix a pallet on the floor here. It would hurt him if I tried to lie on the other side of the bed, I'm sure."

Sarah relayed the news to Catherine as they put their meal on the table. Catherine went to the doorway and said, "Mother, supper is ready."

Goody Dudley came out and sat with them in the kitchen. She eyed the table with approval. "You girls have fixed a lovely meal." In addition to the corn pone, pork, cabbage, and green beans, Sarah had set out the blueberries she had brought.

"We've gathered some bedding for you, Mother," Catherine said. "Do you want us to bring Richard's mattress down?"

"Nay, let Sarah sleep on it. I'll be fine with a couple of quilts."

"Oh, I don't mind sleeping on the floor, ma'am," Sarah said quickly. "I'm used to a hard bed."

A pained expression crossed Goody Dudley's face, and she looked away. "No, my dear. I expect I'll spend a good part of the night in my chair anyway."

Sarah ate in silence, wondering if she had blundered in alluding to the harsh conditions in which she had recently lived. Goody Dudley said no more until she rose from the table and Catherine assured her that she and Sarah would do the dishes.

"Then I shall bid you good night," Goody Dudley said.

"If you need us in the night, call me," Catherine said.

"I shall." Her mother turned and looked at Sarah for a moment. "Thank you for coming. You're a help, that you are, and I'm sure your being here is a blessing to Catherine."

"Oh, it is!" Catherine flashed a smile at Sarah.

"Thank you," Sarah murmured.

She and Catherine hastened to clean up the kitchen then went up to the loft to arrange things by candlelight. Sarah felt a sudden shyness come over her as she entered the sleeping area Richard usually occupied. His Sunday clothes hung from pegs, and a candlestick and a small book rested on a crate beside the bed. She supposed he had taken most of his belongings with him to Canada.

"I know!" Catherine turned, her face alight with excitement. "Let's pull Richard's bed into my room, and we can talk all we want tonight."

Sarah eyed the heavy frame of the rope bed dubiously. "That might be too much of a chore."

"Well, then, I'll bring my feather bed in here and sleep on the floor beside you."

"Let me be the one to sleep on the floor," Sarah protested.

In the end, they decided Catherine's bed was wide enough for two slender young women, and they piled Richard's mattress on top of Catherine's and made the bed up laughing and chattering as they worked. They took off their caps, aprons, bodices, and pockets.

When Sarah sank onto the thick double feather bed in her shift, she thought she'd never felt anything so soft and welcoming.

Catherine blew the candle out. "I'm so glad you came."

"So am I," Sarah whispered. "Are you sure your mother doesn't mind?"

"She's thankful you're here. Why would she mind?" Catherine asked.

"I just don't want to upset her. If she'd rather I didn't. . ."

"Mother has had some dark times, but she knows good help when she sees it. Oh!" Catherine pushed herself up on one elbow. "That was rather crass of me. I meant that even though she may have seemed—"

"It's all right," Sarah said. "I know a lot of people don't like those who've been captive. They don't know how to treat us or if they can trust us."

"Mother doesn't mean to be rude," Catherine whispered.

"She hasn't been. She's been kind to me today, even though she's so worried about your father."

"Sarah, we all missed you. We missed your whole family, if the truth be told. Mother and Father liked your parents, and Molly was a dear. I'm so sorry you lost them."

"And I'm sorry you've lost Stephen."

Catherine sighed in the darkness. "It's Richard I'm fearful for now. What if he and Charles Gardner meet with some accident? Father didn't want them to go, you know."

"We must keep them in prayer," Sarah said.

"Yes. I'm glad Charlie is with him, but. . .even though Richard and Charlie are best friends, and Father respects Charlie, I'm sure, Mother still thinks he's. . .wild."

"Is he?"

"I don't know. They don't let me be around him enough to find out. But Mother has made it plain to me that I'm not to look his way when I begin thinking of finding a husband."

The idea startled Sarah, but why should it? Catherine must be eighteen, past old enough for marriage.

"Do you like Mr. Gardner?"

"Of course. But I'll probably end up with Peter Sawyer or Obadiah Perkins."

"They are more your age, I suppose."

"Boys." Catherine's distaste showed in her tone. "But I expect they'll grow up. Still, Charlie Gardner seems more alluring because so many people won't receive him. It makes him rather mysterious and appealing. I don't really think I'd want to marry him, though."

"Why not?"

"His farm is even farther from the village than ours. The elders nearly forbade him to live out there when he returned. They said he was asking to be raided again. And there's some sort of rule against solitary living. Did you know that?"

"Nay," Sarah said. "He must be brave to live way out here alone."

"I think so, but when I marry, I'd like to live in town, near the trader and other womenfolk. Or perhaps even in Boston."

"Boston?" Sarah refused to think about the bustling city. She felt herself drifting off into pleasant oblivion. "This is like having my sister back," she murmured.

"Thank you! I always wished for a sister. I hoped someday you and Richard. . ."

Sarah's sleepiness suddenly fled. "What about me and Richard?"

"I hoped you'd make a match. We all did."

"Before the massacre, you mean."

"Well. . ." Catherine rolled over; Sarah wondered if she was trying to see her face, but it was too dark in the loft. "I still hope it. He does care for you."

"I'm not so sure about that." Sarah didn't mention the fact that Richard and Charles had stopped by the parsonage and spoken to her before they left the village. That was only for advice on dealing with the Indians. After thinking of little else for several days, Sarah was sure that Richard had visited her only for that reason. He and Charles wanted every advantage, no matter how slight, that they could gain in their search for Stephen Dudley.

Catherine began to breathe with a heavy rhythm, and Sarah turned onto her side, snuggling deeper into the soft bed. Once more she felt herself slipping into sleep. She ought to say her usual lengthy prayers for the Jewett family and Jane and Christine, but she feared she was too tired to make it through the list. "God speed Richard," she whispered.

ten

Sarah and Catherine rose at dawn and put cornmeal on to cook for breakfast. Just as Catherine took up her bucket to head out to the barn and milk the cow, a "Halloo" sounded outside the palisade gate.

Sarah opened the door and called, "Good morning!"

"Morning, Miss. 'Tis Silas Bates, come to do your morning chores."

Catherine pushed past Sarah, carrying her milk pail, and dashed to open the gate. Sarah knew Bates was a farmer who lived in the village and worked his own outlying fields.

He entered the palisade with his hat in his hand and his musket over his shoulder. "I be here to help you, ma'am." He nodded at Catherine; then he looked past her at Sarah and blinked, as though trying to place her and knowing she didn't belong at the Dudleys'. "Parson told us last night about James Dudley being hurt."

Catherine closed the gate behind him. "That's most kind of you."

"How is he?"

"I don't believe he's awakened yet this morning, but when he's conscious, he has a lot of pain."

Bates clucked his tongue in empathy.

"I was just going to milk our cow and feed the ox and the pigs," Catherine said. "If you'd like to do those things, Sarah and I can feed the chickens and collect eggs."

"With pleasure, Miss. Shall I put the cattle out to graze?"

"If you please, sir. Thank you."

Catherine offered her milk pail, and Bates took it and strode toward the small barn at the far end of the fenced yard. He stopped just before entering it and looked back. "Oh, and we'll have a crew of men here Friday morn to cut the hay for your father."

"We're much obliged," Catherine replied.

"It seems the reverend has lined up heavy labor for you," Sarah observed. "Perhaps we can do some baking today, in preparation for the haying crew. They will expect a dinner on the days they work here."

"That's a good—" Catherine broke off and stared out through a gap in the palisade.

"What is it?" Almost as soon as the words left Sarah's mouth, she saw the form of a tall Indian, clad only in breechclout and leggings, on the path outside the gate. Fear gripped her. She would not allow herself to be captured again, no matter what.

Catherine backed away from the fence, her eyes large with terror. "Go away!"

≈

Sarah gulped in a breath and realized that was perhaps not the best manner in which to handle the situation. She stepped closer to the gate and said, "What do you want?"

The man grunted and replied, "Trade."

"You must go to the trading post in the village," Sarah replied. Her heart raced, and she peered through the slit between two of the poles in the fence, wondering if other warriors waited nearby. If a war party were scouting to see how many people were inside the compound. . . She recalled the raids that had ripped her and so many others from their families.

Suddenly she realized that Catherine had left her standing alone by the palisade. Her heart lurched. In the language she had learned in the Pennacook village, she shouted, "We do not trade. You must go to Paine, the trader."

The man's chin jerked up, and his dark eyes glittered as he stared at her. She felt certain that he'd understood her, although his dialect was perhaps not precisely the one she used. Without another word, he turned and flitted down the path toward Cochecho.

Sarah wondered about Richard and Charles and how far they had gone. Seeing the Indian move so freely about the settlement raised questions in her mind. Were the two young men allowed to enter the Canadian villages with as little ceremony? As the warrior disappeared from her view, she prayed for their safety.

Catherine came running from the barn with Goodman Bates behind her.

"Where is he?" Bates panted, raising his musket and pointing it toward the gate.

"Gone toward the village." Sarah leaned against the high fence and pulled in a deep breath. "He said he wanted to trade, and I told him he must go to Paine's."

"Do you think he planned to attack us?" Catherine's dismay still showed in her face.

"I don't know. I didn't see but one man." Sarah's lips trembled as she attempted a smile. "I spoke to him in his own language. I think that surprised him."

"You may have saved us all some grief," Bates said. He scratched his chin through his thick beard. "They go often to the trader, but they don't usually stop at houses along the way. He might have thought you were too far from town for help to come."

"Mayhap you'd best hurry home and check on your own family," Catherine said.

"Aye." Bates peeked out through the gate. "Think ye it's safe to open up?"

Both girls looked out and could see no strangers lurking about. At last, Catherine cautiously opened the gate. Bates went out to stand in the path, staring all about, then looked hard toward his own fields, which were out of sight beyond a dip in the road.

"Both my boys be about the place. I'll finish your milking," he decided and came back inside the fence.

"If you're worried, sir. . ." Catherine began.

He bit his lip then nodded. "I think it's all right. No alarms have sounded. My Joseph would surely have fired the pistol if aught was amiss. And I'd like a chance to speak with your father about the haying when I've finished, if he's awake then."

The girls went about their work, looking often toward the gate and the path beyond, but no more disturbances came to them. Sarah couldn't help thinking of Richard and Charles, wondering if they had met Indians on their journey. Even though she'd lived among them so long, the warrior's sudden appearance had sent a terror through her that still made her tremble as she went with Catherine toward the barnyard where the hens awaited them.

Goody Dudley bustled about the kitchen when they went in with a basket of eggs.

"Ah, there you are, girls. Milking done, is it?"

"Goodman Bates be in the barn," Catherine said. "He wants to see Father."

"James is awake." Her mother stooped to toss another stick onto the fire. "I've got his tea brewing. The leg is powerful sore this morning."

"Mother, an Indian came to the gate a few minutes past," Catherine said.

Goody Dudley straightened and stared at her. "You didn't open to him?"

"Of course not."

"Was he alone?"

"I think so," Catherine said. "Sarah told him to go to the trader."

"Sarah. . ." Mrs. Dudley eyed Sarah thoughtfully.

"Goodman Bates thought it was all right," Sarah said. "And we'd have heard the village alarms by now if there were trouble."

"Yes." Goody Dudley went to the door and stared out toward the path. "Good morning, sir," she called after a moment.

Soon Goodman Bates appeared and handed her the milk pail. "Did your daughter tell you about our visitor this morn?" he asked.

"Aye, she did. What do you make of it?"

Bates shrugged. "They don't often stop and ask for food or a trade at houses anymore. But in the old days, that was common."

Goody Dudley nodded. "Well, times have changed, haven't they? You speak truth, for I remember having savages come into this very room when first we built here. James said let them have what they want for food and perhaps they'll leave us alone. And they did. But that was twelve or fifteen years past, before things got so bad."

"Aye," Goodman Bates agreed. "We thought they would keep peace then. Now we know they're never to be trusted. Is your husband awake?"

Catherine's mother went to speak to James, and then she ushered his visitor into the bedchamber.

Sarah set the table for breakfast while Catherine fixed willow bark tea and cornmeal mush for her father.

When Mr. Bates came back out to the kitchen, he put on his hat and picked up his musket. "If you ladies need anything, you let me know. I think you oughtn't to go outside the fence here without an escort, though. Just my opinion, if anyone cares."

Catherine winced and glanced at Sarah. "We've no one to protect us if we need to go out, sir, not with Father laid up and my brother away."

"Well, I or another man will come by later to do evening chores before dark. If you need aught, you tell one of us, and someone will bring your trifles to you."

"That's good of you, sir," Sarah said.

"Aye," Catherine agreed. "We'll keep close, sir."

He nodded. "Well, I didn't put your cattle out. I didn't like to think there might be savages waiting to butcher them or that you lasses might go out to get them later. Safer to leave them penned up today, I think."

He left, and Catherine carefully barred the gate behind him. The little compound with the house, barn, and kitchen garden seemed smaller to Sarah. She didn't remember this feeling before the massacre, this constant fear. She was as much a prisoner here as she had been in the Pennacook village.

&

Sarah spent the rest of the week with Catherine and her parents within the palisade. Pastor Jewett came twice and brought a small vial of laudanum he'd obtained from the trader. Goody Dudley received it with gratitude and entrusted the parson with a coin and a piece of fine lace she'd tatted to pay for it. She doled it out to her husband when his pain was most severe, especially in the night. Sarah was glad she had it, for Goodman Dudley's moans sometimes awakened her and sent shivers down her spine. She would hear his wife move about quietly in the room below and administer the dose with gentle words. Then he would grow quiet once more, and Sarah was left to her yearning thoughts of Richard and her prayers for his and Charles's safety.

Sarah and Catherine ventured out only once, when the haying crew was in the field, to pick berries in a patch bordering the path within sight of the workers. When the Dudleys' late crop of hay was dried and cocked in the meadow, the men went away with a promise to return when the corn harvest came.

On Sunday morning, Ben Jewett arrived while they were at breakfast. His mother had requested that he escort the young ladies to meeting and back, and to bring Sarah home to the parsonage if she wished to come.

Sarah realized she had enjoyed her stay with Catherine, but she also missed the Jewett family, Jane, and Christine. When she heard that Jane had burned her hand severely while pouring hot water into the washtub, she decided she should go and help out at the parsonage for at least a few days.

Christine and the young Jewetts greeted her with great enthusiasm outside the meetinghouse. Jane had stayed at home with Goody Jewett and little Ruth, but John, Constance, and Abby lined up in the family pew with Christine and Ben. Sarah promised them that she would accompany them home after the service; she explained that she wanted to sit with Catherine, so that she would not be alone in the Dudley pew and feel melancholy.

"Why don't you be a Jewett for the Sabbath day, Miss Catherine?" asked Constance, the four-year-old, looking up at Catherine with adoring blue eyes.

A wide smile burst over Catherine's face. "I never thought of such a thing, but since you have room, I believe I would enjoy it."

She settled in the next-to-front row with the youngsters. Since her return to the village, Sarah had not seen Catherine look so happy. It took only a glance along the row at the scrubbed, eager little faces to remind her what a precious commodity children were on the frontier.

When the services ended, she shed a few tears in saying good-bye to Catherine but promised to visit her again soon. Catherine went off with Ben, her stalwart protector, whose only weapons were a stout stick and a knife, newly acquired as a birthday gift, of which he seemed inordinately proud.

❧

Richard trod quickly along the woodland path behind Charles. Even beneath the spreading trees, the heat of the day penetrated, making his pack feel heavier by the mile. They had been away from home more than a week and had run into no serious problems, although three times they had met Indians. Richard's heart nearly stopped the first time a band of warriors appeared on the path before them. He was sure that only Charles's knowledge of the savages' ways and language had saved them from being robbed or worse.

Now Charles turned around on the path and walked a few steps backward. "Hear that?"

"Aye. Water. Must be a stream ahead." Richard was glad of it. They carried only a small supply of water to save weight, which meant they must replenish it often. So far this had not been a problem, as they came upon fresh, clear streams often, especially in the mountainous territory they had traversed in the last few days. They seemed to be coming down to more level land now, and he hoped their progress would be faster.

Charles stopped on the bank of a small brook and looked all around before getting down to the water. He stooped on a rock and bent to fill his flask.

Richard stayed above, as had become their habit, and kept watch. After a moment, he took off the goatskin water bag he carried slung over a shoulder and tossed it down to his friend. Charles filled it while Richard resumed his sentry duty. When their water supply was replenished, they crossed the stream and settled in the shadows to eat a bit of jerky and a handful of parched corn.

"I expect my corn back home has mostly been eaten by the deer," Charles said, leaning back against the trunk of a large beech tree.

"No doubt they've done some damage," Richard agreed, "but Father said he would see it cut and stored for you." He looked up between the leaves to where the blue sky hung, cloudless. "Do you ever still think about giving up farming and taking to trading?"

"Truly. The venture you and I spoke of so often as boys."

"Do you still want to go to sea?"

"Maybe. Sometimes I feel restless. I'll never have the money for a boat, though." Charles sighed.

"You always used to talk about it, when we were boys," Richard said.

"I know. But now I've gained a new respect for those who till the soil. I'd like to make the farm into what my father envisioned it. He'd only started to clear it when they killed him."

They were silent for a minute, and then Richard said, "My father says I'll have his land one day. I'm not sure I want it."

Charles eyed him in surprise. "Why ever not?"

Richard flexed his shoulders. "What good is it, rooting

yourself to a place, unless you've someone there with you. . . someone who cares about it as much as you do?"

Charles smiled. "Perchance we should go to sea together. They always want deckhands on the trading ships."

Richard studied him to see if he was serious. He decided that Charles had said it in jest, but half to see whether he was serious himself. And if he seized on the idea, Charles would probably agree to sign on with him for a trading voyage. "Nay, I think we're both meant to be farmers."

Charles leaned back against the beech. "Who's to say ye'll never have someone to work beside ye, Richard. Not many days past, we stopped to bid farewell to a handsome young lady."

"If only I could hope again." Richard shook his head and brushed off his hands.

Charles reached over with one foot and kicked Richard's boot.

"Ow! What was that for?"

"You ninny. She's home again, alive and fairly well, I'd say from the look of her. Why should you not hope?"

"I acted badly when they first came." Richard stared down at the dried leaves on the ground. "In fact, I acted so discourteously that I doubt she would ever consider me now."

"Give it time." Charles eased the straps of his pack onto his shoulders and stood. "Come, we've another ten miles in us today, have we not?"

eleven

After Sarah had been a week back at the parsonage, word came that several village men would meet at the Dudleys' the next day to harvest the corn. Reverend Jewett and Ben volunteered to go.

"May I go, Father?" pleaded John, the nine-year-old.

The pastor thought for only an instant before replying, "I don't see any reason against it. A boy your size can pick corn."

"I'd like to go with you, too," Sarah said. "Jane's hand is mostly healed, and she's doing chores again here. I should like to help Catherine and Goody Dudley during the harvesting bee. It will be a big chore to feed all those men a good dinner."

"Oh, let me go, too," Jane begged. "I haven't been past the dooryard except for Sunday meeting these six weeks!"

Sarah was glad to see Jane's enthusiasm and a desire on her part to socialize outside the limited circle of the Jewett house.

The parson looked her over thoughtfully; then he raised his chin and called to the corner where Christine sat in her accustomed place at the loom, "What think ye, Miss Christine? Do ye wish to join Miss Sarah and Miss Jane and venture into the world to feed the workers tomorrow?"

"Nay, sir," came Christine's gentle voice. She didn't look up from her weaving. "I'm content to stay here and help your wife with the children. Perhaps she can rest the morrow, if we've no hot dinner to prepare."

"That's good of you, Christine," said Elizabeth, "but you should go if you want. It will give you a chance to visit with

119

other women for a change."

Christine gave her hostess a placid smile. "I have all the company I could wish for, ma'am."

Sarah knew that Christine's choice stemmed from more than her devotion to Goody Jewett and her concern that the lady would overdo if they left her alone with the three little girls. Christine simply preferred a quiet existence and avoided company whenever she could.

ðŸ™

Ben, John, and their father joined a dozen other men in the Dudleys' fields the next morning, while Sarah and Jane entered the house and found the Dudley women already baking their bread and pastries for dinner. A cauldron of lamb stew simmered over the coals, and the little house was already heated to a sweltering temperature. Sarah and Jane donned their aprons and plunged into the work.

At midmorning, Goodman Dudley called out from the bedchamber, and his wife hurried to do his bidding.

"Father wants to get up," Catherine confided to Sarah and Jane.

"Can he?" Sarah asked, wiping beads of perspiration from her brow with the hem of her apron. "It's only been two weeks since his injury."

"Mother helps him dress, and we bring him out here so he can sit with his leg on a pile of cushions. He wants to be up and ready to greet the men when they come in for dinner."

"That will be good for him," said Jane.

"Aye. He'll want to thank them all and talk over the latest news." Catherine smiled. "Father's tried to be patient while he heals, but he does get restless."

"It will be hard to keep him from going back to his work too early," Jane said.

Catherine went to help support her father, and he limped to the kitchen with her mother on his other side. Once settled in his chair near the door, where an occasional breeze entered to bring small relief from the heat, he closed his eyes for several minutes, his face gray and strained. He roused when Goody Dudley put a cup of willow bark tea in his hands.

"He refused to take the laudanum today," Catherine whispered to Sarah. "He wants to be alert."

A while later, Goodman Dudley seemed to have regained his spirits, and Sarah suspected the tea had taken the edge off his pain.

"Miss Minton, it's good to see you back about the place," he said with a shadow of his former heartiness in his voice. "My daughter amused me with tales of your hard work and collaboration in her adventures last week."

Sarah smiled at him as she sliced carrots into a large kettle. "I enjoyed my visit here with Catherine very much, sir."

"Shall you stay with us now?"

"I am able, if your family wishes it."

"Oh, do!" Catherine bounced to her father's side, grinning. "Sarah is so much fun, Father. She makes work a game, and she showed me how to do lovely beadwork."

Sarah glanced uneasily toward Goody Dudley's ample back, wondering how she had received the news that Catherine was learning to do beadwork in the style the Indians had taught Sarah.

The lady of the house turned from the cupboard with a stack of pewter plates in her arms. "You may stay with us as long as you wish, Sarah. I've not seen Catherine so lively in a long time as when you were with us."

"We had a letter from Richard yesterday," Goodman Dudley said. "Don't know if anyone told you."

Sarah felt a strange sensation in her heart. If it wasn't so warm in the kitchen, she would blush, but her face was probably already scarlet. "Nay, what news?"

"No news, really. He and Charles Gardner met a small group of soldiers on the trail three days out and entrusted a note to them saying they'd got on well and were making good progress."

"We must pray them along on their journey and swiftly home again," Catherine said, and Sarah gave a silent *amen* to her sentiment.

At noon, the harvesters crowded around the table set up in the fenced yard, and the four women ferried the food and tea outside from the kitchen. The pastor and one of the farmers carried Goodman Dudley out so that he could sit in the shade and converse with the men while they enjoyed their dinner.

"I believe we'll get all your corn in today," Goodman Bates said. "A few of us will go tomorrow and take in Charles Gardner's crop, but I misdoubt we can make much of it, he's neglected it so."

"He makes a shiftless farmer," Goodman Ackley noted.

" 'Tis not his fault," Goodman Fowler said. Sarah was glad to hear someone speak up for Richard's friend.

"Aye," said the Reverend Jewett. "Charles was gone three months in the spring bringing our loved ones back from Canada, and now he's undertaken another such errand. We should do all we can to help him."

"May I help again tomorrow, Father?" Ben asked.

"Aye, that you may, and if I didn't have to prepare my sermon for Sunday meeting, I would join you."

From the corner of her eye, Sarah saw Jane slip around the corner of the house. No doubt she feared Ackley or one of the others would begin to make disparaging remarks about the captives.

But Pastor Jewett looked down the table and called in a loud voice, "Ackley, how be your oxen doing? You had much grief training the young one this spring. Is he pulling well with your old Star now?"

&

Though Jane returned home with the minister and his sons that evening, Sarah stayed another two weeks with the Dudleys. During that time, she did much to help the Dudley women dry and preserve their garden harvest to put it by for winter.

It seemed Goody Dudley would never tire of talking about her younger son, Stephen, and her hopes for his return. But when Richard had been gone a month, she became quieter and more grave.

Sarah also heard, largely from his father, how hard Richard had worked to improve the family farm.

"I planned to help Richard obtain land of his own," Goodman Dudley said with a sigh, at dinner one day.

"Do you not think it's best if he stays here with us and you clear more land together?" asked his wife. "With all the Indian scares, we've been a long time putting our acreage into tillage."

"Aye. This place wears down a man," he agreed.

"Richard has always loved boats, Father," Catherine said.

"What's that compared to the soil? If our land had fronted on the river, perhaps he would think of fishing for his living, but that's a dirty, smelly trade compared to farming. A man grows his own sustenance from the earth."

"Or hauls it from the sea." Catherine squeezed her father's arm. "You know your father was a fisherman. You've told me many times how he came from England and lived many years at Marblehead as a fisherman."

"Aye, and lost his life in a storm," said Goody Dudley.

"Well, what is worse, death at sea or death in your field when the savages come through?" Catherine asked, effectively silencing the conversation for a few minutes.

When she rose to take their plates, her mother said, "Well, it is my hope that soon we shall have both our boys back again."

Sarah eyed her carefully and decided she was now accepted enough to speak the truth to her hostess. "I don't wish to dash your hopes, ma'am, but Stephen was so young when he went away. I know captives his age often embrace the Indian ways and consider themselves Indian after a while."

"That didn't happen to you," Goody Dudley said. She turned away to take the plates to the wash pan and fetch the teakettle.

"Nay," Sarah agreed, "I never thought myself Pennacook, though I expect I looked much like them for a time."

"Never," Catherine cried. "With your golden hair and blue eyes? No one could ever think you were a savage!"

Sarah smiled at that. "Nay, my heritage was obvious to all. For that reason, they hid me when strangers came to the village."

Goodman Dudley fixed her with a sympathetic look. "You poor thing. We did wonder about you, whether you lived or died, and if surviving, how you fared."

"It was a difficult season of my life," Sarah admitted, "but the Almighty preserved me and comforted me. I never doubted His care, even if I never had the opportunity to come home."

A sob came from her hostess, and all of them turned to

look at Goody Dudley. When she faced them, Sarah saw tears flowing down her cheeks.

"Forgive me, ma'am." Sarah jumped up and went to the lady's side. "I should not have talked of my life with the Pennacook. It was not my intention to distress you."

Goody Dudley took her hand and squeezed it. "Nay, child. It is not for that reason that I weep. You see. . ." She flung a quick glance at her husband then pulled her shoulders back and continued. "When you returned in May, we counseled Richard to avoid you and give up his hopes of marrying you."

Sarah felt the blood leave her face, and she held tighter to the woman's hand as her knees began to tremble. The idea that Richard still harbored such a thought nearly forced her to resume her seat.

" 'Twas my doing," Goodman Dudley said in a deep, sorrowful tone. "I knew that first day that Richard would wish to claim you, but I feared it would upset our household too much."

"Father, how could you?" Catherine looked from him to Sarah with her mouth twisted in pain.

Sarah's heart went out to the family. Their feelings and grief had been much as she suspected, and in her frequent pleading with God since then, she had fully forgiven their neglect of her.

" 'Twould have upset me, you mean," said his wife. She sniffed then managed a smile at Sarah. "And truly I would have been overset had you come to us that day. It was too much to ask, and I told my husband I could not bear the thought. Although Richard had not spoken of it aloud, I could see by his manner how deeply your return affected him. I tried to put it down to Stephen's not coming home when you did, but I knew it went beyond that."

"Sit down here, ladies, both of you," said Goodman Dudley.

Catherine had kept her place and watched them, wide-eyed and silent. Sarah sat down on her stool and patted Goody Dudley's hand as she took her place in the chair beside her.

"Richard spoke to me openly not a week after your return, Sarah," said Goodman Dudley. "I admit that I discouraged him from acting."

"Aye, to save me the sorrow of being constantly reminded of Stephen's fate," his wife said. "I see now how wrong I was. I can see that you are a staunch, godly, and hardworking young woman. You've brought nothing but good to this house since my husband was injured, and I've seen your sincerity and willingness to give of your strength to help others. It is my wish. . ."

Sarah felt as though her heart had expanded in her chest. As she looked into Goody Dudley's careworn face, she knew she could develop a love for this woman as she had felt for none other but her own mother.

Elizabeth Dudley continued. "It is my wish that you and Richard will make up your differences one day and wed." The lady nodded and looked around at her husband and daughter. "There. 'Tis said. If I've caused offense by speaking so, I beg pardon, but since I so wronged this girl, my heart has pricked me to be forthright about it. Whether you and Richard make a match or not, you are always welcome here, my dear."

Sarah's eyes filled with tears. She slid from her stool toward Richard's mother and was immediately engulfed in a warm embrace. "Thank you," she whispered. "And I shall always love your family, whether Richard comes round to court or not."

Catherine walked around the table and hugged her, as well.

Goodman Dudley smiled benevolently on his womenfolk from the chair where he sat with his healing leg stuck out before him on a cushioned stool. "Well, then," he said, "we shall all pray with one mind for Richard and Charles to return before Christmas with good news."

❧

Goodman Dudley began to do small tasks from his chair, smoothing a new bow for the ox yoke and carving a plug to fit a new powder horn. By the end of Sarah's stay, he was hobbling about on his own inside the house. When he made it to the barn one morning and milked the cow, leaving only the carrying of the pail of milk to Catherine, Sarah surmised she had remained long enough.

"Must you leave?" Catherine cried when she heard the news.

"I mustn't overstay my welcome," Sarah said. She and Catherine poked about the tall grass behind the hen coop, looking for a nest they were sure one of the hens had hidden.

"You could never do that!"

Sarah smiled at the young woman who had now become her dearest friend. "If I go now, you shall be glad when next I come. That is the gift of being not always in one another's company."

Catherine smiled, a bit teary-eyed. "I shall always be glad to see you coming. Always."

"That warms my heart. But Goody Jewett is in such a delicate condition that I'm sure my help is needed there far more than here."

"She has Jane and Christine," Catherine reminded her.

"Aye, and her husband. Let us not forget the many things he does for her comfort. But he has begun writing a pamphlet, and—"

"What about?" Catherine asked. "Is it one of his sermons?"

"Nay, 'tis an account of the massacre and how it affected the people here."

Catherine's eyes widened. " 'Twill sell briskly in this village, I'm sure."

"He doesn't do it for the money," Sarah said, "though I'm sure any extra income would be welcome. He says he does it to help people understand the captives. For that reason, Jane and I and even Christine agreed to let him tell our stories. With him so preoccupied with that and his sermonizing, he has less time for the household. With five children already to look after, and the cooking and washing for a large family. . . Christine already does much, but her preferred employment is weaving or spinning, which is much needed. But you see, there is plenty for all of us to do in that house."

"When I think of all you say, I wonder how Goody Jewett got on before you all came," Catherine admitted.

"She has much on her shoulders," Sarah agreed.

"Are you certain you don't go only to be sure you aren't here when Richard returns? He was dreadful rude to you last spring."

Sarah schooled her face to neutrality as she recalled the day Catherine and her brother came to the Jewetts' house and Richard spoke nary a word to her. She decided not to comment on Richard's behavior. "Don't worry, dear friend. I shall visit you again soon."

The next day, she and Catherine walked to the village bearing Sarah's few belongings, a sack of onions, and several pounds of apples for the Jewetts. Ben escorted Catherine safely home again.

Sarah plunged into the labor of the Jewett home once more with a light heart. All seemed happy to have her back, especially the little girls, and she made it her special duty to occupy them each afternoon so that their mother could have a quiet rest during Ruth's naps, for Constance and Abby had outgrown that ritual.

As she and Jane scrubbed the children's clothes in the yard one September morning, Jane observed, "You are happier of late, Sarah. What has come over you?"

"I'm glad to be back."

"Nay, it's more than that." Jane shrugged. "I thought you would be sorrowful, since young Mr. Dudley has gone off."

Sarah paused in her work. "I try not to fret about Richard. He may meet with some accident, it is true, or he may come home despondent if he cannot find his brother. But the time I spent with his family has gladdened my heart. I'm beginning to see for the first time how gracious God was in bringing me back here and in letting me help the Jewetts and the Dudleys. If I have no more life than this, it is enough. I am content."

Jane eyed her thoughtfully as she scrubbed one of John's shirts. "Are you certain of that?"

Sarah did not answer hastily but considered what her friend asked. Could she truly be thankful if Richard never returned? Or if he returned and failed to pursue their friendship? What if he came home and married another?

" 'Tis easy to say and harder to live out," she said at last, "but I feel in this moment such gratitude that I will say, yes, whatever God brings into my life henceforth, I shall thank Him for."

twelve

The trees that sheltered the trail flamed in red, orange, and yellow splendor. Though the nights were cold, warm days made the journey pleasant, and Richard found it hard to regret his endeavor. He had seen more country than he had ever dreamed of seeing, and he loved it.

Yet this trip made him long to get home to the farm. The harvest must be in now, and fodder stockpiled for the animals. He wondered if his father had done any butchering yet. He should be there to help, but he knew that what he was doing took precedence over any chores he could perform back at the farm in Cochecho.

He and Charles had made good time to the city of Quebec. Charles's previous time in the French colony and his standing as a former negotiator for the English colonies procured them an audience with the governor. Charles had asked for a native guide, but the governor denied this request, saying that surely Charles could find his way to villages he had visited before. Charles took this as an ill omen, but they went on anyway, with their supplies replenished. Their goal was the village where Sarah had lived, which Charles believed to be their most likely starting point.

The faint path led them to a shallow but rapid stream, and they could see where people crossed, relying on rocks that stuck above the surface of the water. The rushing of the stream shut out all other sounds.

As Richard led the way to the far bank, he glanced ahead

and froze, one foot on the last rock in the stream, the other on the dead grass that grew alongside. Two ruddy-skinned warriors stood above him on the bank.

Richard glanced over his shoulder at Charles and gasped. Behind them, on the bank they had left, were three more Indians. He sent up a quick, silent prayer.

Charles grimaced and touched Richard's shoulder. "Easy. Let me pass you."

His pulse racing, Richard hopped back to the larger rock where his friend stood and let Charles ease by and gain the bank. At once he began a conversation with the two warriors that Richard could not comprehend. While they talked, Richard looked back and saw that the others were approaching the same way he and Charles had come. A shiver ran down his spine, and he looked back toward his friend.

"We're going to the village," Charles said.

Richard's anxiety eased only a hair, as the three fierce-looking warriors approached him on the other side.

"Sarah's village?"

"Aye. We're not far. It's as I thought."

"Well, you didn't think we'd have an escort," Richard muttered. He mounted the bank and eyed the party of Indians cautiously. "So, they're Pennacook?"

"Aye. When I told them where we're bound, the leader here said they'll see us to the village."

Richard nodded slowly. The man Charles had indicated as leader was the vilest looking of them all, clad in deerskin breeches, shirt, and moccasins, with a hawk's feather stuck in his scalp lock, a bow and quiver slung over his shoulder, and a knife hanging at his waist that Richard could easily believe had performed many wicked tasks.

The tall warrior's companion went before them, then the leader, then Charles and Richard, followed by the other three. They walked swiftly for two or three miles through the forest. The path skirted a marsh, and at last they came to a river. On its far bank was a village of twenty or thirty bark lodges.

Richard and Charles were herded into separate canoes, and the warriors paddled them quickly across the river. A score of children and nearly as many adults gathered to watch them disembark at the village. The children thronged about them as the men led them to the largest wigwam.

Inside, the smells of smoke and sweat hung in the semi-darkness. Richard paused to let his eyes adjust and was shoved from behind, farther inside the hut.

He made out Charles's figure as his friend took a seat between two warriors near the fire. Several other men already had taken their places, and Richard wasn't able to settle beside Charles as three Pennacook held the spots between them.

A long discourse followed, of which Richard understood not a word. The leader of the party that had brought them in spoke first, relating what seemed an interminable tale to an older man and the others of the village.

Then the old man spoke. And spoke. And spoke.

Richard's throat was dry and raspy from breathing smoke, and his head began to ache. He wondered if he could sleep sitting here, or if it would be advantageous to stay upright and seem alert.

After an hour of this, Charles was allowed to speak. His speech seemed to Richard, in his ignorance of the language, to be quite eloquent. After he'd talked for a few minutes, he brought out a knife and a pouch of tobacco and presented them to the elder. When the man had accepted them with a tiresome speech, Charles took out the letter from the governor of Quebec and talked some more while pointing at the paper.

The old man took the letter, glanced at it, and handed it back. He then started in talking again. Next the warrior who had met them on the trail spoke at length.

Richard's fatigue nearly overtook him, and he caught himself nodding. He adjusted his position and hoped none of the Indians had noticed or thought him rude.

At last Charles squinted at Richard across the smoky fire and said in low but distinct English, "Well, friend, they claim they know nothing of your brother."

Richard's heart sank. "Did you tell them the name Sarah spoke as his Pennacook name?"

"Aye. They say they know not anyone of that name. They say we should leave."

The cruel denial settled heavily on Richard's soul. They could not leave now and go home empty-handed after their long and arduous journey.

"The handkerchief," he whispered.

Charles's eyes narrowed as though he hadn't heard clearly, and then he brightened. Giving a quick nod, he turned back toward the elder and launched a new litany. Several of the Indians spoke in turn; then Charles spoke again, and Richard thought he caught the word *Naticook*, the name of Sarah's onetime guardian. Charles looked expectantly at Richard and held out his hand.

With eagerness, though he was reluctant to give up the pretty thing Sarah had labored over, Richard withdrew the handkerchief from his leather wallet and passed it around the circle to Charles.

His friend took it with respectful mien and held it out to the elder of the tribe.

The old man reached for the bit of snowy muslin and unfolded it slowly. He peered at it then stroked the colorful stitches that made up the flower blossoms in the corners.

Charles began speaking again, and Richard heard the name *Naticook* again.

The elder barked an order, and a younger man left the wigwam.

Nearly a half hour passed before he returned, and in his wake came a wrinkled old woman.

The elder spoke, and the woman drew near the group assembled by the fire. An oration of fifteen minutes ensued before the muslin handkerchief was finally handed round and put in her grasp.

The old woman held it reverently and turned to stare at Charles. He spoke to her gently in her own tongue, and then she rounded and fixed her gaze on Richard. He almost thought tears sprang into her eyes, but the smoke might account for that.

Charles stood and came to where Richard sat. "Stand up," he hissed.

Richard stood, and Charles spoke to the old woman, evidently introducing them. When the woman nodded, Charles said to Richard, "And I present to you Naticook, erstwhile adoptive mother of Sarah Minton."

Richard bowed at the waist, feeling a bit foolish. He should have asked Charles in advance how one acknowledged an introduction to an elderly Indian woman.

Naticook spoke to Charles, and he answered her at length. The woman shook her head, clutching the bit of muslin to her breast.

"What did she say?" Richard asked.

"She thanks you for bringing Sarah's gift and asks us why her daughter left her."

"What about Stephen?"

Charles shook his head. "Nothing."

Richard winced. "Tell her the white chief said Sarah should be with her own people, and she is happy there with those who love her."

Before Charles could relay the words, the tall warrior edged between them and spoke sharply to Charles.

"Come, we must go now," Charles said.

"But—"

"Nay, we must."

"But, Charlie, what about the governor's letter?"

"I showed it to them."

"It's not a request," Richard insisted. "It's an order to tell us anything they know about Stephen and to reveal his whereabouts to us."

Charles hesitated and eyed the warrior as he once more produced the letter and began to speak.

In what Richard assumed to be the utmost incivility, the Pennacook interrupted Charles's plea with a guttural comment, snatched the paper from his hand, and tossed it into the fire.

Richard stared at the burning letter, not quite able to believe what was happening.

"Richard." Charles's voice rose in apprehension.

Richard whirled toward him and saw that the big warrior had drawn his knife.

❧

Two Indians paddled them across the river and left them on the bank. Richard set out, dejected and weary, a few paces behind Charles.

When they had put two miles between them and the river, Charles slowed and waited for him to catch up. " 'Twill be dark soon, but I think we'd best go a few more miles before we camp."

"Charlie, I can't go home like this."

Charles frowned at him. "What more can we do?"

Richard stared at him, unable to believe this was the end. "We could. . . We could find some of their other villages, ask different people. I don't know, Charlie. I don't know." He sank to his knees on the path. "I'm so tired I don't know what to think."

He felt Charles's hand clasp his shoulder. "Come on. A few more miles at least. Then we'll talk and get some rest."

Two hours later, they lay in a thicket shivering and murmuring to each other. They didn't dare light a fire after their hostile leave-taking from the village. Richard's head was no clearer, and neither of them had generated an idea that seemed safe or meritorious.

At last Charles told him, "The elder said they will kill us if we return."

"And you think they mean it?"

"I most assuredly do. Sleep, friend. We can do no more."

Richard tossed for only a few minutes on the hard ground before his body gave in and sleep took him. How much time passed, he did not know, but suddenly he felt a hand on his shin, and he jerked upright with a gasp.

"Charlie?"

"Nay," said a strange voice. "It is Stephen."

thirteen

Richard's steps dragged as they approached Cochecho in a chilly rain. They entered the village, and he caught a glimpse of the parsonage roof. But even thoughts of Sarah could not draw him. He must complete his mission before thinking of visiting her.

Only a few people passed close enough for them to nod in greeting, and he and Charles took the muddy path to the farms together. When they reached the palisade outside the Dudleys' home, they stopped.

"Shall I come in with you?" Charles asked.

Richard shook his head. "I must tell them alone, I think. My mother will grieve anew. Unless—" It suddenly struck him how forlorn a homecoming Charles would have in his cold, empty cottage compared to the welcome he would receive. "Would you stop with us tonight?"

"Nay. You spoke right. Give them your news." Charles nodded. "Come to me in the morn, if you wish to talk."

Richard pressed his lips together and held out his hand. "Thank you, Charlie. You've done more than you ought. You are the truest of friends."

Charles grasped his hand warmly. "You know the path to my door, friend."

Richard watched him over the rise and faced the gate. He drew in a deep breath and blew it out again. *Lord, give me grace one more time.* Raising his voice, he called, "Father! Be ye within, Father?"

Through a crack between the posts of the fence, he saw Catherine leap down off the doorstep and run toward him. She threw off the bars, swung the gate open, and flung herself into his arms.

"Where's Father?" he asked as she nearly strangled him with her embrace. "It's nearly dark. Is he yet at the field?"

"Nay, he's within. Oh, Richard, come inside and tell us all!"

He slid his pack off his back at the door and shuffled in after her. His family had been at the table, and the remains of supper lay still in evidence. The smells of fresh bread and stewed chicken made his stomach rumble.

Richard hurried to kiss his mother. To his surprise, his father did not stand to greet him.

"You will pardon me, son, but I do not get out of this chair until I have to nowadays."

Richard stared at him, surprised that in three months his father had taken on the attitude of an old man.

"Father broke his leg," Catherine said, "but it's better now."

"Much better," his father agreed. "Sit down, boy."

Richard removed his coat and sat down heavily on a stool next to his father. "How did this happen?"

"Later," his father said gently. "We've time to talk of that. Tell us of your adventures."

Richard took the chair his mother set for him by the hearth and shook his head as he stared into the glowing fire. "I never should have gone."

He saw that they all watched him with sorrow ready to spill over in tears, for his returning alone had said the news for him. He swallowed hard and steeled himself for the added pain he was about to inflict on those he loved.

"We found Stephen."

"What?" His mother jumped from her chair and seized

his arm. "Where is he? Richard, what—" She stopped and studied his face; then she slowly dropped her hand as her face lost its animation. "Tell us."

"We got to the village where Sarah had been, and they kept us a long time talking. Charlie showed them the letter we got from the governor of Quebec, but that didn't seem to sway them. We met the woman in whose home Sarah lived while she was there, but she had nothing to tell us, either."

"How horrible was it?" Catherine asked with a shiver.

Richard smiled. "Let us just say it is good to be home. Very good."

"But. . .how did you find him, if they kept quiet and would not aid you?" his father asked.

Richard nearly laughed, for he would not have described the long-winded Pennacook as quiet. But he sobered as he remembered the night that followed. "We didn't find him," he said softly. "He found us."

His mother gasped.

Richard reached for her hand and eased her onto a bench beside the fireplace. He unfolded the tale of how Stephen had learned of his presence before Richard and Charles had entered the village. "The warriors who escorted us in had, unbeknownst to us, sent a runner to another village not far away, where Stephen now resides. But he came not near while we were in the camp. Or if he came, he didn't show himself. After we'd left, however. . ." He sighed. "They drove us off. Told us to go or they would kill us. And the chief threw the governor's letter in the fire."

"Oh, wicked," Catherine cried.

Richard nodded. "At first I tried to talk Charles into looking further, but he assured me the savages would keep their word and slay us if we persisted. I gave up hope then. And so we went. But Stephen. . ." His chest felt as though a giant hand squeezed it, and he closed his eyes for a moment. "He followed us several miles without our having a suspicion anyone was there and watched us crawl into a thicket in the dark and settle down for slumber. And then he came and woke me."

Every eye was fixed on him, but no one spoke.

"He told me he could not come home with me. He said he was. . .better off to stay there." Tears flooded Richard's eyes, and he wiped them with the back of his hand. "He truly believed that if he came back here, everyone would hate him."

His mother's tears flowed freely as she whispered, "Did you not tell him how we love him?"

"Aye. But he is a man now, among the Pennacook. He hunts with their men and—" Richard caught himself before *fights with them* slipped out. He looked around at his family and gave them a bleak smile. "He said he cannot come back to this world and he doesn't want to try."

"But what have they there for him?" his father asked. "A hut made of branches, a life of hunting and starving and freezing?"

"I know." Richard bowed his head. "He refused to come and threatened Charles and me if we tried to follow him or if we ever came back to his people."

Catherine began to sob.

"I told him that you were all well and thinking constantly of him and wishing him home."

"What did he say?" his father asked without hope.

"That we must stop thinking so. He will not come."

Goody Dudley burst into tears, and though Catherine hurried to console her, her own sobbing nearly drowned out her mother's.

"Come, son," his father said after an interval of tears and deep thought. "Take your boots off. Have some supper. You, at least, are home now."

◦

The next day, Richard plunged into the work of preparing the farm for winter. Many tasks lay undone because his father had not liked to ask his neighbors to neglect their own work to do his. Catherine and her mother had toiled, and James Dudley had done all within his meager power.

But the supply of fodder for the livestock was less than it would have been if he'd retained his full strength and had his son to assist him. Richard would have helped him harvest more hay from the salt marsh and perhaps even glean a meager third cutting from the meadow. A few of the palisade posts needed reinforcing, and a leak had developed in the barn roof. Besides all this, James decided to butcher four pigs, leaving only two that would need winter feed.

For several days, Richard worked from dawn to sunset, racing winter. One light snow had already fallen before his return but had not stayed long on the ground. But on the fourth day after his return, snow fell heavily as he walked to the barn in the early gray light of morning. He fed the animals and had just sat down to milk the cow when the barn door swung open. He turned toward it and saw his friend in the doorway. "Charlie! What brings you out in this?"

"I thought you might need an extra hand today. Tomorrow is the Sabbath, and you've much to do this day, I've no doubt, before your enforced rest."

Richard grimaced and kept milking. "You must forgive me, friend. I meant to come to you, but I've been so caught up in my work here that I broke my word."

"Nay," Charles replied, leaning against the post where a low wall separated the cow's stall from the rest of the small barn floor. "I've no livestock, and my little corn was put up for me, so I hadn't much to do. How goes all with your family?"

"Father was injured soon after we left. Did you hear?"

Charles shook his head. "I've seen no one these four days."

"He had an accident involving a middle-sized ash tree. He's been all this time recovering and still moves slowly."

"I do hope he's not done permanent damage?"

"He says not, but at his age. . ." Richard stripped the cow's udder and set the pail aside.

"What is your intention for today?" Charles asked.

"If this snow lets up, I thought to begin cutting firewood for next year. The ground is frozen hard now, and the snow will allow for dragging the logs out." Richard stood, picked up his milking stool, and hung it on the wall outside the stall.

"I shall help you."

"We'll work together, then. But if the storm be too harsh, we'd best wait it out." Richard looked out the door of the barn. The snow fell thick and fast. "Catherine and Mother plan on shelling beans today. If it's too foul for me to work outside, I expect I shall help them."

"Then I shall help, too."

"Had you any beans?" Richard asked.

"I fear the groundhogs and deer got them all."

"Mother tells me we have plenty. I'm sure she can spare a share for your help."

"That is not—"

"Oh, hush," said Richard.

Charles came to stand beside him in the doorway. "How is your mother taking the news about Stephen?"

"She is distraught and yet more controlled than I expected. She and Father—aye, and Catherine, too—are relying on their faith to sustain them."

Charles nodded. "That is the best course, for we have done all in our earthly power."

"Aye." Richard drew in a deep breath as he stared across the dooryard toward the snug little house. "Charlie, Cat told me Sarah Minton spent much time here in my absence."

"Oh?"

"She came with the parson as soon as they heard Father was injured. And she stayed and helped Mother and Cat for some time."

"That can't be bad."

Richard shook his head, but he couldn't quite bring himself to look into his friend's eyes. What if he saw there the teasing laughter Charlie used to shower on him when they were lads?

"I. . .feel a change in their thinking. About the captives, I mean. Especially about Sarah."

"As I said, that cannot be bad. I rejoice with you."

Richard puffed out a breath. That achy longing had returned. "Hold off on celebrating awhile. But you're right. It is something. It is. . .a great thing. Mother in particular has come far in this attitude."

Charles squeezed his shoulder. "Have you seen her yet?"

"Nay. I've anticipated the Sabbath and tomorrow's meeting. But. . ." Richard looked out at the snow, now more than two inches deep on the ground. "If this keeps up all day, we'll not make it to meeting."

"Do not give up hope this early, my melancholy friend. More likely this storm shall end ere noon, and we'll break the path with little trouble."

Richard sagged against the door frame. The falling snow had, if anything, increased its density and speed of falling.

"I think I understand her better now, Charlie. How she feels, and how difficult it has been for her to return to this community."

"There is hope," Charles said softly. "Much hope. Come, let us clean up your byre and go and help the ladies shell beans."

fourteen

On Monday morning, Sarah set out after breakfast with Ben Jewett. Few people had come out for meeting on Sunday, but of course she, Jane, Christine, and all the Jewetts had attended. Only hardy people who lived in the village proper had made their way to the meetinghouse in the midst of the storm.

The snow had continued until midday on Sunday, leaving about eighteen inches of frozen fluff on the ground. At dawn Monday, men could be heard urging their oxen to drag heavy boards through the town to scrape the street.

"I hope the path is broken," Sarah said to Ben as she hurried along behind him carrying a basket. She had stout leather boots now—the Reverend Jewett had insisted that all the young ladies have sturdy footwear for winter, and the trader had donated one pair and given the others at cost. A thick woolen cloak of Goody Jewett's wrapped her snugly. The wind had died, and the sun sparkled on the snow, giving the illusion of warmth. Indeed, Sarah fancied the snow had already begun to melt from the rooftops.

"If it's not, then we shall break it," Ben assured her. " 'Tis only a mile."

Sarah smiled at his optimism. She was glad for his company. Ben had walked with her and Jane many times now, escorting them on their errands about the village. At thirteen, he had surpassed her in height and begun to show downy whiskers on his chin.

The trail was scraped only as far as the first two houses

beyond the village, and after that there were only boot tracks where several persons had taken the path. Ben preceded her and stomped down the snow between the footprints. It was slow going and strenuous work, but Sarah reflected that the exertion was no doubt good for them both.

She wondered if she would learn any news about Richard today. She doubted he was home, though. When he returned, he would almost certainly pass through the village, and she expected he would report to the reverend on the outcome of his mission. Still, the snow had blocked many people from their purpose these last two days. At any rate, she would spend the day doing what she could to cheer the Dudleys. She'd brought a loaf of Jane's rye bread and was prepared to recite the main points of Parson Jewett's Sunday sermon for the family.

They were nearly halfway to the Dudleys' farm when they saw three young men sitting on a stone wall that edged one of the farmers' cornfields. No doubt these were the ones who had started to break the path, and Sarah was disappointed that their way would now be harder. She recognized two of the three—Felix Maybury and David Tucker. The third boy she had perhaps seen at meeting but didn't know his name.

Ben stopped suddenly, directly in front of her, and she came up short.

"What—" She broke off as the scent of acrid smoke hit her nostrils.

Ben turned and stared at her with huge blue eyes. "They're *smoking*!"

From beneath the edge of the shawl that covered her head, Sarah peered at the three young men then pulled her eyes hastily back to Ben's face. That Felix had a pipe in his hand there was no doubt. When she glanced back his way, he'd hidden it behind him, but the warmness of the air belied the thick cloud of his breath when he exhaled.

Sarah gulped down her surprise and realized that the boys' misbehavior was more shocking to Ben than it appeared to her. After all, the Pennacook, both men and women, had often smoked Indian tobacco in her presence.

"Just ignore them," she whispered.

Ben eyed her for a long moment then turned back to his task. They stomped along, and when they reached the spot where the young men had veered aside to the stone wall, he renewed his vigorous trampling of the snow.

Sarah noted that his face was red, and she feared hers had gone scarlet, as well, knowing the three watched them from where they lounged on the wall. She wondered if they realized she and Ben knew what they were doing or if they cared. Even as the thought flitted through her mind, she saw Felix slip the pipe to David, and David put it to his lips.

"Sarah," Ben hissed.

"Don't pay any mind to them. Come, I'll take the lead for a while. You must be tired."

They were barely a dozen yards past the end of the boys' trail when Felix called out behind them, "Say, young Jewett! Be you squiring ladies about town now?"

Ben opened his mouth, and Sarah whispered, "Answer him not, Ben! Come!" She turned her back to the young men once more and plodded through the deep snow, not bothering to stomp a path. The cold at once struck her as her feet plunged deep, and the snow closed in over her boot tops.

"Ladies?" The young man she didn't know guffawed.

"Oh, pardon," said Felix. "Methinks I should have said 'females.'"

David Tucker stood up and yelled, "Hey, Ben! Is that your squaw woman now?"

Sarah gasped and turned toward them. Ben had a stricken look on his face.

"What do you say, Ben?" Felix called. "Aren't you afraid she'll scalp you?"

Ben lowered his gaze, and his lip trembled.

Movement beyond the boy drew Sarah's eye, and she pulled in a breath. Felix Maybury was plowing through the snow toward them. Before she could speak, he had reached them and grabbed her arm.

"Well, now, Ben, that's a pretty sweetheart you've got, though she has been tarnished."

"I'll wager she's a wild one," David laughed. He, too, had left the wall and had passed half the distance toward them.

"Let go of me!" Sarah jerked her arm from Felix's grasp, stepped backward, and overbalanced. She slipped backward and fell into the snow, her cheek slamming against the edge of her basket. She floundered to sit up.

Ben leaned to offer his hand, but Felix shoved him away. "Get back, puppy. I'll help the *lady*." Felix spoke the last word with such contempt that Sarah's blood ran cold.

Sarah rolled over in the snow and pushed herself up, facing away from Felix, but she felt his hand on her shoulder before she'd regained her feet. "Don't touch me," she snapped.

When she turned, she saw that David was holding Ben back and the third young man was coming to their assistance.

"We'll hold this mewling pup," David said, nodding at Ben. "Steal all the kisses you like from the wild woman."

Ben struggled, and David punched him. Sarah tried to pull away from Felix, but his grip on her shoulder clamped tighter.

A sudden shout from farther up the way startled them all, and Sarah swiveled toward the smooth, unbroken trail ahead. At the top of a rise fifty yards away stood a tall man in a thick woolen coat with a knit hat pulled low over his brow. Behind the long barrel of the musket he held pointed at them, she saw the hard, dark eyes of Richard Dudley.

❧

Richard advanced toward them quickly, in spite of the deep snow. His tall leather boots kept the snow out, and his long legs made little of its hindrance. He kept the musket leveled at the young men, choosing to aim at Felix, the one who seemed to be the chief offender.

"Hey, Dudley," David Tucker said, releasing Ben and falling back a step. "We were just helping these two. They got out in the deep snow and was floundering, like."

"Quiet, Tucker." Richard advanced nearer, focusing on Felix's face.

Felix seemed to realize suddenly his posture and let go of Sarah. She stepped away from him, closer to Ben.

"Well, Dudley," Felix said. "Didn't know you was back from Canada. How's your father? Is his leg mended now?"

Richard stopped three paces from Felix and stared at him down the barrel of the musket. Disgust filled his heart as the young man attempted to appear innocent before him. "If you ever touch this woman again—"

"You'll what?" Felix's question was more of a challenge.

David and the other young man backed stealthily away, but Felix stood his ground. "Next you'll be defending savages," he sneered.

Sarah and Ben were now several paces from any of the others, and Richard moved quickly. He flipped the musket end for end and swung it at Felix, catching him solidly on the chest with the maple stock and knocking him backward, where he sprawled in the snow, gasping for breath.

Richard lowered the musket and took a few steps toward him. Panting, he looked down at Felix. "As I said, don't ever lay a finger on her again. Nor any other young lady in this town."

David and the other boy turned and pelted for town, leaving their friend to haul himself erect and stumble after them.

Richard stood watching with narrowed eyes until they were out of sight. Only then did he turn and look Sarah and Ben up and down. Sarah looked fine, though her face was pale. "Be you still in one piece?" he asked.

Sarah nodded.

"Aye," said Ben with a grin. "You laid him flat, Richard!"

Richard eyed him critically. "Your eye is going all purple. Won't your mother be pleased!" He looked back toward the path once more. "I'll have the constable on them within the hour. Tucker, Furbish, and Maybury."

"Furbish?" Sarah asked. "So that's who he is."

"Aye. Goodman Furbish's eldest." *His father will not be pleased*, Richard thought.

Ben sobered. "I'm sorry, Sarah. I was supposed to protect you."

"Three on one is not a good match, Ben," she said.

He was not consoled but frowned up at Richard. "Think if there *had* been Indians."

"No, don't think it," Richard replied. The idea of losing Sarah again was beyond the realm of bearable thought. "Where are you headed?"

"Your father's house," said Sarah. "I thought to visit your family. We'd not heard you were home yet."

"Aye, but work and weather have kept me from the village."

She held his gaze with blue eyes full of concern and hesitation. When she turned to include Ben in the conversation, he remembered they had an audience in the boy, and many things he wished to say could not yet be discussed.

"Ben, you needn't go all the way to the Dudleys' with me now if you don't wish to," she said.

Ben looked apprehensively toward town, and Richard wondered if he thought the rowdy young men might lie in wait for their return.

"Or perhaps. . ." Sarah faced Richard in confusion. "Perhaps there is no need for me to go, since you are back. You could take my gift to your mother." She held out the basket.

"I'm sure they would wish for your company more than whatever delights you've prepared for them," Richard said, "if indeed you still wish to go."

"Oh, I do." Sarah averted her gaze.

Relief warmed him, routing the momentary disappointment he'd felt at the thought of leaving her now and not spending time with her as he'd planned. "In truth," he said, "my object this morning was to visit you at the parsonage. If you are not too fatigued, we could walk with Ben and rest a bit at the Jewetts' fireside and then go on out to the farm."

She looked at the boy. "Would that suit you, Ben?"

He nodded, looking from her to Richard and back.

"And I could bring you home safely this afternoon before nightfall," Richard said hastily.

"Thank you. That sounds like an agreeable plan." Sarah wrapped her cloak closely about her and surrendered the basket to him.

On their short trip back toward town, Sarah and Ben up-dated him on the recent events in the village. When they arrived at the Jewetts', Goody Jewett and the children swarmed around to greet them. Ben's black eye brought nearly as many comments as Richard's return, and after a few minutes, Goody

Jewett sent John to the meetinghouse to fetch his father.

"I can't countenance this," the pastor said as he eyed Ben's face.

"You don't think they would have seriously harmed them, do you?" his wife asked anxiously.

"From where I stood, it looked sinister," Richard told them, "and I acted as such."

"Shame, shame!" Goody Jewett wrung her hands. "Boys of our village. 'Tis unconscionable."

"Sarah, I must ask you and Richard to delay long enough to give the constable your story," the minister said.

They removed their cloaks and mittens and sat down to wait while the Reverend Jewett went to the ordinary to summon the landlord, who was also the constable.

Mr. Oliver clucked his tongue and shook his head repeatedly as Ben and Sarah then Richard recounted what had happened on the trail. The parson demanded that he arrest the young men and put them in the stocks. Oliver assured the Jewetts that the three miscreants would be brought before the magistrate and punished.

At last they were allowed to go, after Sarah received many admonitions from Jane and Goody Jewett and a silent hug of support from Christine. Richard gave her his hand as she negotiated the doorstep, but she released it as soon as she stood on the path.

They set out again on the snowy trail. Richard marveled at the silence and beauty of their surroundings compared to the noisy, crowded room at the parsonage. Sarah inhaled deeply and looked all around at the snow-laden evergreens and sparkling fields.

They walked in silence for some time, Richard with his musket and Sarah carrying the basket once more. Richard began to tell her of his journey with Charles, his elation when he met his brother at last, and the sorrow that followed.

Sarah shed no tears when he told of his meeting with Naticook. "I'm glad you saw her, and I am not surprised that she offered you no aid in finding Stephen. But neither would I be surprised if I learned she was one of those who told him of your presence."

Richard thought about what she said for a short distance then shared his thoughts with her. "Sarah, I learned some of what it meant to you to be there in that place so long. You must have been terrified."

"One cannot remain in a state of terror forever." Her smile was tinged with sadness. "Of course I was frightened at first, especially on the journey north, not knowing what would befall me. But after I'd been in the village a few months and began to feel that I wouldn't be torn out of there again, but would remain in comparative peace, I felt less anxious."

"And Naticook was kind to you?"

Sarah's eyes crinkled a bit. "I wouldn't say *kind*. She was not cruel, though occasionally she swatted me with a stick if she thought I did not move quick enough. But my lot was no worse than anyone else in the village—and better than some."

When they had passed beyond the place where the young men had accosted her and Ben, she looked up at Richard. "I haven't thanked you properly."

"No need," said Richard. "I'm only glad I came along at the right moment."

" 'Twas not the way I imagined our next meeting."

"I am flattered that you imagined it."

She smiled and trudged along with him. They had reached a stretch where only his boots had broken the snow, and the going was much more difficult. She soon fell behind and stepped in his tracks, while he quickly trod down a better path for her.

They arrived at the Dudleys' home without further mishap and told his family of the morning's events.

"Those wicked boys must be punished," Catherine cried.

"Fear not," Richard told her. "The parson will not rest until it is done. They'll be in court for assault next time the magistrate comes."

Sarah dove into the work the women had started that morning—shelling corn. His father was helping, too, and Richard despaired of having more time alone with Sarah.

"You might as well go and cut more wood on this fine day," his father said.

"Nay," said Catherine. "Not while Sarah is here to visit us."

"Guests mustn't stop the work of the household," Sarah told her.

Richard stared at her. True, he didn't often give up a fine day when he could be out working, but after all, he had planned to do so today, at least for the morning, with the express object of speaking to her. Of course, they'd had half an hour on the way here alone, but still he felt he'd been cheated.

His father rescued him by pointing to the corner, where Richard had left his ax on Saturday evening.

"Mayhap your tools need sharpening before you can spend another day in the woods."

This suited Richard's mood, and with a little thought, he was able to find several tasks that kept him inside and near Sarah.

The five of them passed several pleasant hours in conversation, and Goody Dudley was even able to speak of Stephen without breaking into sobs. "I shall never forget all you and Charles did for us, Richard," she said after Richard had given another retelling of his story. "I know you needed to settle in your own heart whether Stephen lived or no—"

"And whether he lived with the savages of his own accord," Catherine added.

"Well, yes. But as I was saying, I know you did it for yourself, but you also did it for all of us, and for that we thank you. I would never ask you to undertake such an ordeal, but since you did, you have given me peace."

"Peace, Mother?" Richard asked. "Indeed, I've seen great change in your manner since I returned, but I did not expect you would be in peace now."

" 'Tis God's peace," she told him, and a single tear slid down her cheek. " 'Tis not my peace, but He tells me all is well, and I must trust Him."

❧

With an hour of daylight left, Sarah and Richard donned their wraps. Sarah kissed her hostess and Catherine good-bye and thanked them for their hospitality. Her heart filled with affection, for she knew she had been accepted into the family circle without reservation.

As they set out for the village, Richard shouldered his musket. The air had warmed even more throughout the day, and he left his mittens hanging out of the pockets of his woolen coat. Sarah fancied the snow had shrunk several inches in depth since that morning, and the path seemed far easier to tread.

"We'll soon have you home," Richard said. "Let me take your basket for you."

"Nay, 'tis not heavy—only a skein of yarn Catherine pressed upon me so that I can knit a cap for the new babe."

Richard's cheeks colored above his beard, and Sarah realized she'd become accustomed to speaking freely about Goody

Jewett's pregnancy to the women she most often associated with.

"Pardon," she murmured.

"Nay, no need."

They walked on for a few more steps in silence, and Sarah ventured, "Catherine spins the finest yarn I've ever seen. I plan to dye it yellow before I make the—" She broke off in confusion as Richard swung round in the path and stopped, facing her. Had she said something amiss?

"Sarah." He looked down at her, his dark eyes roving over her face, seeking. . .what? His gaze settled in again on her eyes, and she wished he would tell her what went through his mind in that moment.

"Richard?" she whispered.

His look softened, and he reached for her with his free hand, still holding the musket pointing skyward with the other. He touched her face, and his big hand felt warm against her cheek.

"I love you, Sarah."

She caught her breath and gazed up at him. This was a moment she had waited for these five years and more. She couldn't help smiling.

He stooped and brushed his lips against hers, and Sarah longed to throw her arms about him. Still, they were out in the open, where anyone might see, and such actions might be considered lewd behavior.

Richard apparently had other thoughts, as he drew away from her and stared carefully all around at the trees.

"Come," he said, putting his free hand to the butt of the musket. "We mustn't linger here."

They soon reached the place where the path met the village street, and Sarah walked beside him up the hill to the parsonage. With every step, her heart soared and her thoughts cast about for the right response to his declaration. Just before they entered the dooryard, she took a deep breath and slowed her steps.

"Richard?"

"Aye?"

They stopped and looked at each other. Sarah inhaled sharply, knowing he mustn't protract his stay in town if he wanted to reach home before dark.

"I. . ."

The door of the house opened, and John and Ben bounded outside.

"I feel the same way," she murmured.

The boys charged toward them, shouting a greeting. Richard laughed and let them chatter away, commenting on how Ben's bruises had spread into a fine proof of his mettle. John had a tale to tell of snaring a rabbit that day for the first time.

When they reached the door, Sarah glanced at Richard with an apologetic smile. "Shall you come in for a moment?"

"I do wish to see the parson." His significant look stopped her in her tracks, and a warm prickling spread over her.

"Father be visiting the relict Woolsey," Ben said.

"Ah. Then I shall walk that way and perhaps meet him," Richard said. He glanced up at Sarah, who now stood on the door stone. She thought the color in his face was higher than their walk in the cool air warranted. "I'll. . .see you again soon, Miss Minton."

She smiled. So formal in front of the boys! It was so unexpected that even Ben stared at him, though John took no notice. "Aye. Thank you for bringing me."

He nodded, shook the boys off, and headed toward the widow Woolsey's cabin with a pronounced spring in his step.

fifteen

The next morning, Sarah thought the pastor and his wife seemed especially cheerful—if not jubilant. At breakfast, the minister reported that the three young men who had assaulted Ben and Sarah would face the magistrate within a fortnight and were under close watch by the constable in the meanwhile.

This good news did not seem enough for the knowing smiles the couple exchanged or the beaming looks bestowed upon Sarah. She could not deny the joy and expectation that simmered within her, and she had little doubt the Jewetts' mood had something to do with that, as well.

Confirmation came soon after, when she settled near the hearth with Christine to mend clothes for the entire family. Sarah chose a shirt of John's and prepared a patch for the torn elbow, while Christine sewed a button on the parson's Sunday waistcoat.

"I wish you joy," Christine murmured, her head bent over her task.

"Oh?" Sarah asked. "And what is the occasion?"

"Goody Jewett mentioned this morn that you will be leaving us soon."

Sarah lowered the material and needle to her lap and eyed Christine with mock severity. "If it's true, then I know none of it. Shame on you for gossiping so."

Christine let out a soft chuckle. "We remarked when you left yesterday, Jane and Goody Jewett and I, how Richard looks at you now. And something must have passed between him and the reverend last night. Pastor said before us all at supper that Richard had gone to Goody Woolsey's to speak to him."

"But he did not divulge his errand," Sarah pointed out.

"Oh, surely it is known to you."

"I am surprised at you, Miss Hardin," Sarah said in the most stilted tones she could muster without laughing.

Christine's face colored. "I mean no offense. I'm truly happy for you, if this is what you wish."

Sarah picked up her sewing and took a few stitches around the edge of the patch. "I was teasing, Christine. If Richard's intent is what you think, then, yes, I believe it is what I wish, and I think I'm ready now."

Christine reached over and squeezed her hand. "I shall never marry, but I'm truly pleased for you. He is a fine young man."

Sarah wondered if Christine would change her mind one day. Perhaps, if the right man came along. . . She also wondered how she would contain her disappointment if their assumption proved false and Richard's conversation with Pastor Jewett had nothing to do with her future.

The daylight hours dragged as she watched the children and baked bread. After the noon meal, she helped the boys stack a load of firewood that one of the parishioners brought in his wagon for the parson. In midafternoon, the Reverend Jewett came home from studying and broke in upon the household with a burst of energy.

"Children, come! Get your sleds. The snow is perfect, and we shall join the Tuttles and the Otises for a sledding party."

Sarah and Jane scrambled to help the little girls get their wraps on.

"Ruthie, too," the pastor said, tossing the toddler into the air.

Ruth squealed in delight, and Christine left the loom to bundle her up in cap, mittens, and coat.

Ben and John by this time had the sleds ready outside the door, and the pastor eyed the young ladies with a challenging smile. "Come, Jane, Christine. Stretch your legs."

"I shall stay with your wife, sir," Christine said.

Sarah thought he would bow to her excuse, as Goody Jewett was within two months of her lying-in and seemed to grow more fatigued each day.

But Pastor Jewett gave her a sly look. "Nay, I've picked Sarah for that duty. She shall keep Elizabeth company, and all shall be quiet here. Perhaps my wife will have a nap."

Sarah felt a moment of disappointment, for she had not been sledding in more than five years, and the thought of rushing down the hill with one of the children appealed to her. But as soon as the thought came, she noticed the pastor's meaningful look at Christine, and she almost thought he winked at the shy maiden.

At just that moment, a deep voice hailed the boys outside, and all became clear in Sarah's mind. Richard had come calling, and her guardian was clearing the house of all the children and the other young women, leaving her alone with his wife to entertain Richard in a measure of privacy.

She felt a flush suffuse her face, and she hadn't yet laid eyes on him. The pastor hustled his daughters and Jane outside, and Christine, the last one out, pulled the door to behind her, shutting out the greetings and chatter from the yard. Sarah looked to the hearth, where Elizabeth sat in the armchair her husband had made her.

"Do you mind, Sarah?" the lady asked.

"How could I mind, with your company, dear Goody Jewett?"

"Oh, I doubt my company shall be of much consequence." Elizabeth smiled gently. "If you feel the same way as you did a few months back and don't wish to accept any man's addresses. . ."

Sarah bowed her head for a moment. Elizabeth was right. She had felt and said those things just a short time ago—that she didn't wish to marry and perhaps never would.

"Perhaps God has healed your heart," Elizabeth suggested.

"Aye." Peace washed over Sarah as she let that knowledge settle over her, and she returned Elizabeth's smile.

A solid rap came at the door—not too bold, yet not timid or tentative.

Elizabeth arched her brows at Sarah and nodded toward the sound. "I believe you have a caller, my dear."

Sarah tossed her apron aside and smoothed her hair as she took the few strides to the door. No time to consider the disorder of the room. The caller would have to understand the chaos that attended a large family, especially when all had bustled to prepare for an unexpected outing.

She opened the door and stood eye to eye with Richard. A giddy anticipation shot through her as their eyes met. His lips curved upward, transforming into a blinding smile.

"Sarah."

"Aye. Welcome, Richard." She stepped back to allow him room to enter and closed the door behind him. In her mind, she cast about for the next logical phrase. *What brings you?* Nay, too bold, when she knew. *How is your family?* perhaps.

Elizabeth saved her the trouble. "Good day, Richard. You will forgive me for not rising to greet you. I tire so easily these days."

"Please do not bestir yourself," he replied, stepping forward and offering Goody Jewett his hand.

"I shall stay right here with my knitting, if you do not mind, and you and Sarah must make yourselves comfortable. Let Sarah take your coat, and bring a bench nearer the fire."

Richard obliged and loaded another log onto the coals before he sat down next to Sarah. "Too near the flames?" he asked as she rearranged the folds of her skirt.

"Perhaps a bit." She stood and let him move the bench back, wondering if he felt as nervous as she did.

They sat in silence for a long minute, both of them watching the fire.

"How is your family?" Elizabeth asked, and Sarah almost laughed with relief.

"They be fine." Richard inclined his head toward Goody Jewett. "Father's leg grows stronger, and he's helping with morning and evening chores now. Mother seems more at peace. She and Catherine be making cheese today."

Elizabeth nodded. "Sarah told me that you saw your brother in the north."

"Aye. 'Twas not what we wished, but 'tis better than not knowing whether he lives or nay."

" 'Tis God's blessing to allow you to know," Sarah said softly.

Richard threw her a grateful smile. "I believe so," he said.

The two of them continued to talk quietly after that, and Sarah found it not difficult after all. After about ten minutes, she glanced over and saw that Goody Jewett's eyelids drooped and she had let her knitting fall into her lap. She wondered if she ought to offer to help her lie down on the bed, but perhaps that wouldn't be proper with Richard here.

He touched her hand, and Sarah jumped. When she looked up at him, the tenderness in his expression chased all thoughts of propriety from her mind. She did no more than flex her fingers and suddenly her hand was cradled in his; then he leaned close to her.

"Sarah, my dearest, I pray you have forgiven my lapse when first you returned. I deserve every rebuke you gave or thought to give me."

"Nay," she answered, breathless. " 'Twas unjust of me to scold you. I think time was needed for all of us to put events in their proper place."

He nodded, and his dark eyes seemed to blaze, though perhaps it was only the reflection of the fire. "I love you, Sarah, and I can't go a waking hour without thinking of you. Please would you—can you—consider being my wife? I would do all within my power to protect you and provide for you."

She caught her breath. "Aye," she whispered.

"We would have to stay with my family the winter," he rushed on, "but Father and Charlie Gardner will help me build us a cabin in the spring. It won't be fancy, but I'd make sure it would be solid and keep out the rain and snow, and Father says I might be able to acquire some land, though we haven't much money. But—" He stopped and stared down at her for a moment as though just taking in her response. "You. . .will?"

"Aye. 'Twould fulfill my greatest desire on this earth," she managed.

He exhaled, closing his eyes for a moment. Then his eyelids flew up, and he darted a glance toward Goody Jewett, who seemed to have dropped into a doze, slumped in her chair.

"Sarah. . ." He slipped his arms around her and drew her toward him. "If you don't think it improper. . ."

"I don't."

He kissed her then, and Sarah was bold enough to slide one hand up into his soft beard. Richard held her firmly against him, and all her anxiety fled, except one fleeting fear that Goody Jewett would suddenly rouse and see Richard passionately kissing her ward.

Indeed, as soon as he drew back, he glanced once more at their hostess, but she had not stirred. He then lingered with his arms about Sarah, which encouraged her to dare rest her head on his shoulder as they resumed their study of the fire.

≥•

At the Sunday meeting, the Reverend Jewett preached a fine sermon. Sarah sat up front with Jane and the children. Christine again had remained at home with Goody Jewett, who now found it beyond her strength to walk up the hill to the meetinghouse and sit for several hours on a hard, backless bench.

Richard sat several rows behind her, she knew, but she kept from looking back. If she met his gaze, her face would surely betray her feelings. No use giving the villagers more to gossip about.

As the sermon drew to a close, the pastor entreated the people to forgive and be compassionate to one another. He read a short section that Sarah was certain came from his pamphlet, urging the people to accept as brothers and sisters those who returned from enforced servitude in a foreign land.

"And now, brethren," he cried, "I bid you join me in seeking to show greater compassion and charity. If you commit to treat thus those within the church, stand before God and man, pledging on your honor to do your part in making this a better community."

Sarah stood and heard many move behind her as the bulk of the congregation rose. For several seconds, a stirring was heard as others got to their feet. She supposed a few did not, or perhaps stood only out of shame, seeking not to be one of the few who refused to comply with so reasonable a request.

The pastor raised his eyes at last and offered a prayer of thanks for the unity of spirit among the people. When the prayer was done, instead of dismissing them, he said, "Please be seated. It now gives me great pleasure to read to you the marriage intentions of Richard Dudley, goodman, of this parish, and Miss Sarah Minton, also residing here."

As he read on through the banns announcing a marriage to take place in a fortnight, a murmur reached her ears, which she knew were scarlet now as the blood rushed to her face. It seemed a favorable, hopeful wave that swept the congregation.

When they were dismissed, she helped bundle up the little ones again, and they wended toward the meetinghouse door, where the pastor greeted each member as the people left. As they descended the steps outside, she noticed with a rush of joy that Richard waited at the bottom.

"Might I walk you home?" he asked.

Sarah looked over her shoulder at the parson, who was just descending the steps with Ruth in his arms. He bestowed a cheerful nod on them, and Sarah allowed Richard to draw her mittened hand through his arm as they proceeded toward the parsonage.

&

A week later, Richard whistled as he set about his evening chores. The weather had turned cold, but that could not dampen his spirits. In a week, Sarah would be his wife. Catherine walked past the door of the byre with a basket on her arm, and he knew she went to feed the poultry. He tossed fodder into the ox's feedbox and sat down to milk the cow.

"Richard!" His sister ran into the warm, dim byre, panting for breath.

"What is it?"

"An Indian. At the gate."

"That's odd. You'd think if they meant us harm they wouldn't come up to the gate openly. Did he speak?"

"Nay. I saw him approaching as I went to the hen coop, and I ran to fetch you."

Richard rose and set his milking pail and stool where the cow could not reach them. "The gate is properly barred?"

"Aye. This happened before, while you were gone."

"Oh?"

"Sarah was here," Catherine said. "She spoke to the man in his own tongue, and he left."

Richard nodded and took a hay fork from where it hung on the wall. "I shall see what he wants. Go to the house and tell Father. He'll get his musket."

Cautiously he crossed the dooryard. He could barely make out a dark figure through a slit in between the logs of the palisade. The man was just outside the gate. Richard glanced toward the house and saw that Catherine had gained the doorway. He wished he had a better weapon than the two-tined hay fork.

A foot from the solid gate, he stopped. He couldn't see the warrior now, though he knew he was there. His heart beat fast, and he tightened his grip on the handle of the fork. "Good day," he called. "What do you want?"

"To see my mother."

Richard felt as though his chest were being squeezed by a giant. He rested the fork on the snow and reached for the bars; then he drew back his hand. "Stephen?"

"Aye, Richard. Your brother."

Richard closed his eyes and leaned against the gate. "God be praised," he whispered. He opened his eyes and threw the hay fork aside then hurried to remove the bars. When the gate swung open, he beheld the young man he had only seen in darkness on the trail.

Stephen, at nearly sixteen, was almost as tall as Richard, but thin and wiry beneath the deerskin clothing he wore. On his feet were moose-hide boots and short snowshoes. His dark hair was pulled back and liberally greased, and he carried a leather pouch, a bow, and a quiver, slung over his shoulders.

Richard realized Stephen was staring at him, as well, no doubt taking in his bushy beard and his knitted mittens and warm woolen clothing. He was glad he had set aside the hay fork.

"Richard!" his father yelled from behind him. "Everything all right?"

Richard didn't take his eyes off Stephen but called, "Yes, Father."

His brother's eyes darted past him and flared as they focused, no doubt, on his father.

"Welcome home, Stephen." Richard opened his arms wide.

Stephen looked at him in momentary confusion; then he slowly stepped forward into his embrace.

❧

Richard paid a visit to Sarah two days later and begged her to walk out with him. Goody Jewett was happy to give her an errand at the trading post, and they set out together.

As they left the house, he looked down at her, noting with sweet anticipation how a lock of his future bride's golden hair glimmered in the sun where it peeked from beneath her hood.

"I'd say I've thought of nothing but you these two days," he told her, "but that would not be true. Much as I delight in seeing you, Sarah, I must give you the news."

"What is it?" She looked up at him with apprehension.

"Our family is set on its ear. Stephen has returned."

She puffed out a breath that turned to white vapor in the cold air. "When?"

"Two nights past. I was doing my chores. Catherine saw him at the gate and thought he was a Pennacook."

"Oh, Richard! How wonderful. And after he'd told you that he wouldn't come."

He nodded. "We were all stunned." He struggled for the words with which to express to her his joy and turmoil. "Sarah, he told me that since he'd seen me he couldn't stop thinking about me. I'd told him how Mother prays for him every day. Indeed, we all do, but Mother especially, and that seemed to get hold of his heart. He says he began to wonder what a mother's prayers could do."

"God used it to turn his thoughts," Sarah breathed.

"Aye, you say right. He wept when Father took him in his arms. And the look on his face when first he saw Mother, I can't describe to you. But he's wild. He can't sleep in the house, and he's restless all the time. Wants to get out beyond the fence, where he can see a long way off."

"Have you put him in the loft, where he can see over it?"

"Nay, he insists on sleeping in the byre. I think the house constrains him. But he says for now he is comfortable with the cattle. Which is odd, don't you think?" He gazed down at Sarah's sweet face, searching for reassurance. "I mean, the Pennacook don't keep cattle, do they?"

"Seldom. But he probably wants to be where you can't see him. Or mayhap the sounds of others or the smells of cooking and such keep him awake."

"Did those things bother you when you came back?"

"Nay, truthfully, what bothered me most was a soft pallet to sleep on. Your sister's feather bed was even worse, but I enjoyed every moment of lying in it."

Richard laughed. "I hope he will be at our wedding."

"He will stay, then?" Sarah asked.

"We don't know yet, for sure. He hasn't said as much, and we're hopeful that he's not putting off a decision to leave us."

"That would be better than his deciding now to go."

"Aye, but. . .Sarah, I thought perhaps, in the spring. . ."

"What, Richard?"

He looked deeply into her eyes. "If you disagree, I shall not press the matter, but I thought we might offer him a room in our new home."

She nodded. "I don't mind. But I didn't think we would have such a large house to begin with."

"Father and I have been talking, and we think three rooms below and a large loft above. It's not safe to build a little cabin with no upstairs. You need to be able to look down on anyone approaching without. And we'll fence it all about, of course."

"Shall we live near your parents?"

Richard shrugged. "I had thought to build next to Father and extend the palisade, but a parcel of land is available between us and Gardner's. Our house would be between Father's and Charlie's. I suppose we could build closer to Father, on his land, but. . ."

"Nay, we should live on your property, if you are able to secure it," Sarah said firmly. "Richard, it will be good to have your brother with us, if we're to be one of the farthest houses out from the village."

"Aye, my thinking, as well. He told me he is glad to be home, but he feels a bit stifled. If he lives with us, he can come and go as he pleases. You would understand his discomfort better than my mother does."

"I am agreeable. But perhaps he would like to build his own wigwam, or a little cabin away from us."

Richard nodded. "I will tell him you suggested such. If he is content to stay, he shall always be welcome."

She smiled up at him. "Come. We have an errand to fulfill, and I see Goody Paine watching us closely."

"She's harmless," he said with a laugh, "but you are right. We must proceed, or I would stand here in the street all day talking with you and forget my business."

epilogue

In the chilly little parsonage of Cochecho, Richard Dudley pledged his love to Sarah Minton in late November, and the Reverend Samuel Jewett solemnized their vows. All the young Jewetts stood gravely by, and Elizabeth sat in her armchair, alternately smiling and weeping. Jane Miller and Christine Hardin also witnessed the ceremony, both seemingly deep in thoughts of their own.

With Richard came his family. They had set out early that morning, the slow but faithful ox pulling his parents in the sled while Catherine, Stephen, and Richard plodded along through the snow behind.

It was Stephen's first appearance in the village, though the pastor had visited the Dudleys' home during the week. Few people saw his arrival at the parsonage that day, and fewer still recognized the tall young man. He looked much different than he had when he presented himself at the Dudleys' gate, for by his request his mother had cut his hair. She and Catherine had altered some of his father's clothing to fit him, and he now looked to be a respectable colonist.

At the conclusion of the vows, Richard bent down to kiss his bride, and all gathered close to wish them well. Jane and Christine began to serve the cake they had prepared and hot chocolate, a luxury provided by Richard's parents. Goody Dudley had brought extra dishes in the oxcart so that all could partake together.

Stephen stood aloof at first, but the parson drew him into

conversation, and soon Ben and John approached, as well, eager to hear anything Stephen would tell about his former life.

After an hour of good company, the Dudleys prepared to make the journey back to the farm.

Jane came to hug her, and Sarah whispered to her, "Beware of the pastor and his wife's matchmaking."

"Should I? More than previous?"

Sarah smiled. "It's just that I saw a look pass between them."

"What sort of look?" Jane asked.

"You know the one I mean. One that says, 'We've done it! One safely home, and two yet unmatched.'"

Jane smiled. "Now that you speak of it, they do seem proud of this day's work. I shall be forewarned."

Richard brought Sarah's cloak and held it for her. "Well, wife, will you ride in the oxcart with my parents?"

"Nay," she said with a smile. "I shall walk with my husband, my sister, and my brother."

He reached for her hand and plunged it, clasped in his, into the deep pocket of his coat and whispered, "Homeward, then, my love."

A Letter To Our Readers

Dear Reader:

In order that we might better contribute to your reading enjoyment, we would appreciate your taking a few minutes to respond to the following questions. We welcome your comments and read each form and letter we receive. When completed, please return to the following:

Fiction Editor
Heartsong Presents
PO Box 719
Uhrichsville, Ohio 44683

1. Did you enjoy reading *Return to Love* by Susan Page Davis?
   ❏ Very much! I would like to see more books by this author!
   ❏ Moderately. I would have enjoyed it more if

   _____

   _____

   _____

2. Are you a member of **Heartsong Presents**? ❏ Yes ❏ No
   If no, where did you purchase this book? _____

   _____

3. How would you rate, on a scale from 1 (poor) to 5 (superior), the cover design? _____

4. On a scale from 1 (poor) to 10 (superior), please rate the following elements.

   ____ Heroine   ____ Plot
   ____ Hero   ____ Inspirational theme
   ____ Setting   ____ Secondary characters

5. These characters were special because? _____

_____

_____

6. How has this book inspired your life? _____

_____

_____

7. What settings would you like to see covered in future
   Heartsong Presents books? _____

_____

_____

8. What are some inspirational themes you would like to see
   treated in future books? _____

_____

_____

9. Would you be interested in reading other **Heartsong
   Presents** titles?   ❏ Yes   ❏ No

10.   Please check your age range:
   ❏ Under 18   ❏ 18–24
   ❏ 25–34   ❏ 35–45
   ❏ 46–55   ❏ Over 55

Name _____

Occupation _____

Address _____

City, State, Zip _____

WYOMING
Brides

3 stories in 1

In the wilds of old Wyoming, three women face insurmountable dangers. Can they trust the Lord to preserve their love through the trials of life in the wilderness?

Historical, paperback, 368 pages, 5³/₁₆" x 8"

_____

Please send me _____ copies of *Wyoming Brides*. I am enclosing $7.97 for each. (Please add $3.00 to cover postage and handling per order. OH add 7% tax. If outside the U.S. please call 740-922-7280 for shipping charges.)

Name_____

Address _____

City, State, Zip _____

To place a credit card order, call 1-740-922-7280.
Send to: Heartsong Presents Readers' Service, PO Box 721, Uhrichsville, OH 44683